THE
FLAPPER

THE FLAPPER

Stories, Poems and Dreams

SUSAN KNIER

iUniverse

THE FLAPPER
STORIES, POEMS AND DREAMS

iUniverse books may be ordered through booksellers or by contacting:

iUniverse
1663 Liberty Drive
Bloomington, IN 47403
www.iuniverse.com
844-349-9409

ISBN: 978-1-6632-1790-5 (sc)
ISBN: 978-1-6632-1791-2 (e)

Print information available on the last page.

iUniverse rev. date: 01/30/2021

What though the radiance
Which was once so bright
Be now for ever taken from my sight,
Though nothing can bring back the hour
Of splendor in the grass,
Of glory in the flower
We will grieve not, rather find
Strength in what remains behind

-William Wordsworth

"Hope" is the thing with feathers-
That perches in the soul-
And sings the tune without the words-
And never stops – at all-

-Emily Dickinson

Hey hey! Charleston Charlie
He's so jolly
He sure does know his stuff
He never gets enough
Women praise him 'cause he's rough
He never worries
Never hurries…

-"Charleston Charlie" from
Bert Firman and His Orchestra

STORIES

RADIO SIGNALS

My weekdays were spent as a buyer for Millman's Department Store. But my weekends were spent as a buyer of antiques and vintage items. I was in my element at estate sales, thrift shops and antique malls. On that warm, windy October Saturday, I had driven to Prairie du Chien in western Wisconsin to an antique store. I was looking at glassware and several hats from the 1940s when I saw it, perched alone on a table draped with lace – a cathedral radio.

I approached it almost reverently, admiring the rich mahogany finish and the cloth speaker. I was so far away in my contemplation that I didn't notice the store proprietor standing next to me, a wizened elderly man with preternaturally bright blue eyes. He was sucking on an unlit pipe.

"1933 Philco cathedral radio," he began. "That's the original cloth speaker – completely intact. I heard about the attack on Pearl Harbor listening with my daddy on a radio just like this." He motioned for me to step closer to the radio and pointed to a round area near the top of the radio that I initially thought was an extra tuning dial or power button.

"This here's something called a 'magic eye.' When a station was completely tuned in, the magic eye would open all the way. If the eye was slitted or partially closed, you needed to fiddle with the dial to tune it in better."

He stepped back and continued, whistling softly through his teeth. "This one had it all...AM, medium wave, short wave. I remember listening to the BBC in London on our radio, just like it was ten miles away!"

"How much?" I blurted.

The man was still for a moment. "Well, ma'am, it's a gorgeous piece. The externals are in unusually pristine shape but…and this is a big 'but'…" The man gently turned the radio around to reveal only a stub of a power cord. "It was brought in this way. Someone cut away the power cord, so this radio will be forever silent. It isn't like the later transistor radios where you can pop in a battery."

I was still sold. "I don't mind!" I replied. "I just love it!"

That evening I arrived home to my condo in downtown Milwaukee. I placed the cathedral radio on an antique sewing table in my bedroom. I could not stop admiring it. Radios were beautiful and grand pieces of art and furniture back then, I mused. Radio was the glue that bound the world together before the advent of television and the information superhighway of the Internet. I thought about people clustered around this very radio in the distant reaches of the past – laughing and being entertained or finding out that their lives would be irrevocably changed via the scourges of war…

My entire body felt weighted down with fatigue when I turned the key in the lock after work that following Tuesday evening. After a quick microwave dinner in the kitchen, I retired to bed and fell into a coma-like sleep.

About 3 AM, I woke up ravenously thirsty. Too much sodium in those microwave meals I thought as I returned to my bedroom with a glass of water.

Then I noticed it. The dial on the cathedral radio was backlit! I walked over to it, wondering if it was a trick of the moonlight. The backlight on the dial promptly went off when I was about a foot away from the sewing table.

"Impossible! Not happening!" I whispered. I peeked in back of the radio, noting the stub of a cord. I nodded and went back to bed.

"Ruthanne!"

I was staring into space as my co-worker Connie called my name at work the next day. She was waving her hands in front of my glassy eyes on the other side of my cluttered desk.

"Earth to Ruthanne! Golly, girl, you are a million miles away!" Connie crowed.

"I'm sorry. I'm just tired. Now what did you say?"

Connie sighed. "For the tenth time, I said that corporate needs a decision on the cable knit sweaters by 3 PM CST! Got it?"

"Yep. I'm on it."

But my mind was on the cathedral radio.

That night, my eyes went back and forth between the digital clock on one side of the bed and the cathedral radio on the other. At 2:37 AM, I decided to get up and channel surf in the living room as sleep seemed a distant prospect. I settled on an infomercial for a miraculous spot removal product, hoping that abject boredom would culminate in sleep. There was a brief lull in the strident sales pitch to flash several ordering options on the screen, just long enough for me to hear it.

It sounded like static.

Coming from the bedroom.

My legs were shaking as I returned to the bedroom. Had I set the alarm incorrectly, perhaps tuned between stations instead of to my usual oldies station? But it was as I feared.

The cathedral radio's dial was again backlit but now static emanated from the cloth speaker.

I crouched down, initially paralyzed in thought. I timidly reached out to the tuning dial. The magic eye was closed, true to the shop proprietor's comment regarding its use as a tuning aid. My quivering fingers moved the dial slightly to the left and right. The dial was surprisingly responsive, as if well oiled.

Then I heard it.

Voices!

They were ever so faint as if the station was nearly out of range of the intended listening area. The magic eye remained shut.

I knelt down and placed my ear close to the cloth speaker. The volume knob was turned all the way up but the voices were still faint and nestled in static. Despite these obstacles, I could unmistakably hear two voices – a man and a woman. I could even discern that they were speaking English. I held my breath to further eliminate any background noise.

"This stew is cold!" The man sounded extremely irritated.

"I – I'm so sorry, John. Here, I'll heat it up again-"

"Get your hands off my plate, Rebecca! Don't touch my food! You hear me? Can't you do anything right? I've been up since before dawn milking cows, plowing, fixing that infernal truck and you can't even make a suitable dinner!"

I winced, feeling like an uncomfortable eavesdropper. I continued listening as Rebecca profusely apologized again for the temperature of the stew and later for the insufficient quantity of the stew for this hard-working man. Rebecca then began to cry. John's escalating shouting began to be replaced by an electrical humming coming from the radio speaker. I was disappointed because their voices became inaudible. Shortly after that, the backlit dial became dark and the speaker silent.

I sat down on the carpet in shock. What had I just heard? Or what had I just witnessed? Was this play-acting – like the old serial soap operas that came forth from this radio in its prime? Or was this an actual, very real conversation?

I stood up and absently touched the radio. The beautiful wooden case was warm to the touch.

Two nights passed without incident. I slept fitfully. When I awoke each time, the digital clock displayed the time in large blue numbers and the cathedral radio stood in darkness. All seemed right with the world again.

That is, until the next night.

I had come home from work with a gargantuan headache. It was 3:08 AM and I had just returned to bed after dosing myself with another couple of Tylenol when the static started again.

I kicked the covers off and rolled across the bed to the cathedral radio. I stood over it, head pounding. The dial was again lit, displaying 937 kilocycles. The faint voices again emanated from the speaker. After several seconds, I could tell that it was once again Rebecca and John. The volume was extremely weak. I tried tilting the radio this way and that to improve reception but to no avail. I would have to resign myself to listening very carefully.

"Who was that man you were talking to on the porch this afternoon?" John was clearly antagonized already.

"Oh, he was looking for work."

"What did you tell him?"

"That we were fine and didn't need anyone at the moment."

There was a pause. I could hear the clinking of cutlery again. They were obviously having another meal.

Finally John spoke. "You know what I really think?"

"Yes, John honey, what?"

"I think it was more than that!" John was shouting now.

"What?! John! It was nothing more! You've got to believe me!" Rebecca's tone was pleading now.

"Maybe you'll tell me the truth now!" John howled. I could hear what sounded like a dish breaking.

"Please, John! Don't! That's my mother's wedding china! Please!" wailed Rebecca.

The voices stopped. All I could hear then was the sound of dishes and perhaps glasses also breaking as Rebecca wept.

It was then I decided that this was not a broadcast drama. This was real.

I took a long walk during lunch the next day at work. Rebecca was now a real person to me and she needed help. She needed to get away from John. But how could I help her? I knew nothing about them or where they were. I didn't know a surname to do an Internet search on them. I couldn't communicate with Rebecca; thus, I probably couldn't help her. I felt a bleak sense of failure as I returned to the revolving door at the office.

It was 12:15 AM and I had just had my third round of espresso. Even though I wasn't sleeping well lately, I didn't want to take any chances on missing a transmission from Rebecca and John.

At 1:54 AM, they returned. The volume of the transmission was still frustratingly low so I pressed my ear to the speaker. John was already on a rant.

"Where is it, Rebecca?" he howled.

"I don't have it, John!"

"Two dollars vanished into thin air, just like that? You think I'm stupid, do you? Where did you put it?"

"John, honest, I didn't take it! It should still be in the cookie tin in the cupboard above the icebox!"

Icebox? I was a bit puzzled by the antiquated reference but I kept listening intently.

"Maybe this will help you with the truth!"

I jumped back as a smacking sound came through the speaker,

disproportionately louder than their dialogue. This sound repeated itself several times until I heard a slamming door. I cringed. I actually felt Rebecca's pain and fear. Now all I could hear was Rebecca's crying.

I felt entirely helpless to the point of near insanity. Then I had an idea…a long shot, to be sure. But I had to try! Rebecca had just had quite a beating and John wasn't likely to stop in the future.

"Rebecca!" I yelled into the speaker.

She continued weeping.

"Rebecca!" I shouted so intensely I had to stifle a cough.

Then the crying stopped. My heart literally began to sing as she timidly said, "Hello? Is someone there?"

"I'm here! I'm here!" I bellowed.

There was a long pause as static predominated. Then, "Who is this?"

"I'm Ruthanne Dexter, Rebecca. I'm a friend. I want to help you. Are you all right?"

"I think so. I can stand but my eye hurts."

I continued to shout and overarticulate. This might be the most critical conversation of our lives.

"Okay, Rebecca. I need you to call the police. Right now!"

Another pause. "We don't have a phone. The nearest one is in town."

I was so confused then that it was an effort not to get sidetracked. "Okay, Rebecca, is John gone?"

"Yes. When he's mad, he gets a bottle and stays out all night."

I was overjoyed. Perfect! "Rebecca, I'm coming to get you. What's your last name?"

"It's Millner. M-I-L-L-N-E-R." Her trust in me showed that she was truly at rock bottom in her options.

"Where do you live?" I grabbed my cell phone to upload the GPS.

"Highway 37 and Divine Road. Southeast corner. Near Elkader, Iowa." She clarified, "About 35 miles outside of Elkader."

My heart was pounding as the location loaded in GPS. It was almost 2:15 AM. I could make Elkader in about three and a half hours, but I needed a more specific address. When pressed for one, Rebecca said she didn't know anything about where she was beyond what she already told me and began to cry again. I reassured her and told her I would be there at dawn.

I turned off my headlights as dawn broke. I realized that Elkader wasn't too far from Prairie du Chien where I'd acquired the radio. Coincidence? I was definitely in the farmbelt as I traveled down Highway 37. The cathedral radio sat beside me in the passenger seat. I had opted to take it along so I wouldn't miss any further transmissions.

I felt like I'd been on Highway 37 for near forever when I saw the sign for Divine Road. My heart sank as all I saw was an open field. There was a small weathered corn crib with a mossy collapsed roof in the far corner. I parked the car on the shoulder. A large dairy farm was across the road, but Rebecca had been very clear that she was on the southeast corner.

I picked up the cathedral radio in my arms and began to pace the field in imaginary "rows," like a search party grid. I prayed for another transmission. Was it too late? Was this a hoax? My mind ran wild and then-

The cathedral radio sprang to life in my arms. I was so startled I dropped it into the field grasses. The dial lit up and this time the magic eye was wide open. An angry male voice blasted through the speaker as clear as a 50,000 watt radio station across the street: "YOU'RE TOO LATE! SHE'S ALREADY DEAD!"

I wailed and covered my ears as the radio went dead. Then I began to kick the radio in anger...anger against John, anger against Rebecca's helpless position, anger against the universe... I began jumping up and down on the radio, smashing the beautiful mahogany cabinet. My feet then became entangled in the torn cloth speaker and I fell on my back to the cold ground.

When I looked up, two uniformed police officers were looking down at me with a mixture of fear and concern.

I was briefly detained and questioned back in Elkader. Police contacted the current owner of the property in Florida and he declined to press trespassing charges. I was released after a psychiatric evaluation and advised to seek counseling locally.

As my shock and embarrassment subsided, I returned to Elkader for research and some closure. With the kindly assistance of the Elkader librarian, I pieced together the story of John and Rebecca Millner. Public records showed that they were indeed real people. John A. Millner purchased a 3 acre farm at Highway 37 and Divine Road outside of Elkader in 1933. He lived there with his wife, Rebecca P. Millner, until 1935. The farmhouse burned down with John in it that year. Rebecca then moved to Abilene, Texas. Further research demonstrated that Rebecca co-founded the "Hope And Care Women's Shelter" in Abilene in the late 1960s. According to the obituary, she died "peacefully at home, surrounded by her family" on August 2, 1990 at the age of 90.

I had completely misinterpreted that final radio transmission. She had indeed died, but after a proud, productive and peaceful life, loved by others! I also found it interesting that the male voice on the final radio transmission had not been John's.

I then leaned back in my chair at the Elkader Public Library, looking at one final part of Rebecca's obituary on the microfilm viewer.

Her photo.

She was up in years in the photo. Her tender, grandmotherly smile was an embodiment of kindness and gratitude.

A small scar remained, barely visible, just beneath her left eye.

THE LESSON

I stood with my fists curled on the front steps of my home. The school had called earlier to tell me that my son Colton was being suspended for three days, effective immediately. He had been caught verbally bullying a new student who recently moved here from the Philippines with her family. Apparently her cleft lip repair and struggling command of English inspired my son's cruelty.

There he was, lazily ambling up the walk in his private school blue blazer with the Riverdale Academy logo emblazoned on the breast pocket. He had already loosened his tie. His navy blue dress pants were slightly too long and overspilling his shoes. He wielded a backpack heavy enough to stoop his shoulders a bit. Colton's cheeks were flushed as he crept past me into the house, immediately depositing the backpack onto the floor.

"Get your sorry butt in there!" I rasped, motioning him to go into my home office. I looked at Colton in disgust. Why was I forking out all of this money for a private high school when my son behaved like a boor? As I sat behind my desk, I made a mental note to consider transferring Colton to public school in fall. However, Riverdale Academy had a "zero tolerance" policy regarding any form of bullying. After Colton's suspension, my wife and I would meet with the principal to discuss next steps, including potential expulsion. So my public school idea may not be so far off after all.

Colton stood on the other side of my desk, cheeks still flushed and his face reflecting a mixture of insolence and boredom. Of course. He simply couldn't be bothered with any of this.

"Sit down." This was stated as a command to him.

I steepled my fingers together in thought. After a considerable pause, I began. "Colton, I've been thinking about how to punish you. I thought about assigning extra chores around the house, but you always seem to worm your way out of those. I also considered grounding, but that becomes like a vacation after a while with a built-in excuse to sleep in every day. So the only thing I could come up with is this. I am going to tell you a story. It's something that happened to me as a boy. And you are going to listen."

Colton's eyes were vacant with abject boredom as I began.

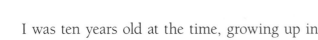

I was ten years old at the time, growing up in a loving family in Long Beach, California. My dad Pete was a plumber and my mom Carol ran the household. I was in the fifth grade at U.S. Grant Elementary School. The school year had just begun with that vibe of happiness and excitement that inevitably fades away after a few weeks.

I noticed a new kid in my class. Actually, it was difficult not to notice him because he had a prosthetic arm. Most of the other kids just stared at him but Lonnie, Scott and Devon were relentless in making fun of him. (Actually, Devon would hang in the background looking this way and that while Lonnie and Scott did the actual "dirty work" of bullying. He acted like he couldn't wait for it to be over but then he stayed with the pack. I wondered if he was truly on board...)

"Cyborg! Freak!" Lonnie crowed at the new kid.

"Freakshow!" added Scott with gleaming eyes.

The new kid would remain calm and motionless, just waiting for it to be over. He seemed comfortable in his own skin to a degree that many adults are not. His face was preternaturally peaceful and pleasant during the bullying as if it was nothing hurtful or unusual. I was intrigued.

I saw him at lunch on a day that Lonnie and Scott had been

particularly vicious to him, including putting one of his gym shoes in the toilet. He was calmly eating alone at a table by the window, far away from the mob in the cafeteria. I walked over with my brown bag and sat down across from him. He looked up from his sandwich with a momentary expression of surprise that quickly reverted back to his default calm mode.

"Hi," I opened.

"Hi," he replied.

"I'm Matt."

"Hi, Matt. I'm Aidan."

"You're new here."

"Yup, my mom and I just moved here from Omaha. That's in Nebraska," he added helpfully.

"Oh," I said, tearing off a chunk of the gigantic ham sandwich my mom had packed for me.

Aidan's arms were propped on the table in relaxed fashion as we chewed. I noticed that his prosthetic left arm bent at the elbow, just like a natural arm. The prosthesis was in a flesh tone that was a bit lighter than Aidan's natural skin, but not a bad imitation.

"Got any brothers and sisters?" I continued.

"Nope."

"Me neither. Grandpa and Grandma?"

"No, just me and my mom."

My eyes went back to Aidan's prosthetic arm. "How did it happen?" The question escaped my mouth before I could fully think about it. My mom and dad always warned me about that – think before you speak!

Aidan briefly looked down at his prosthetic arm as if to tacitly say, "Oh, you mean this?"

"The doctor found a tumor in my arm. He took it out and I got better."

Oh, simple as that, I thought. "Did it hurt?"

"I don't remember. I was only three years old."

"Oh."

"Then the cancer came back in my arm. This time it got into the bone. It was going to spread all over, the doctor told my mom. So the doctor cut my arm off."

I was speechless. I had so many more questions. Aidan spoke as if an amputation was just part of the routine, like brushing your teeth.

"Hey! What do you do after school?" Aidan's topic shift was lightning quick.

"I usually play basketball. My dad put up a hoop on the garage."

"Oh, I like basketball, too. Hey, have you ever played pinball?"

"No!"

"No?!" Aidan seemed shocked, as if I'd told him that I didn't require oxygen. "You're kidding!"

I had seen pinball machines many times at the arcade with their fancy designs, chrome and levers, but I had never played. I usually stuck to video games like "Pac Man" and "Space Invaders," or I tried my hand at the shooting gallery.

"You gotta come with me! There's this place – Metzger's Pharmacy. At the back, there's this awesome pinball machine. You need quarters to play. It doesn't take anything else. Can you go?" Aidan was beaming.

"I want to, but I have to talk to my mom first. If she says okay, how about tomorrow after school?"

"Great!" Aidan took my phone number and wrote it on the inside cover of his spiral notebook, promising to call me tonight to hear the verdict.

Of course, my mom said yes. Aidan called right before bedtime, yelling "Cool!" and "Remember to bring quarters!"

As we walked to Metzger's Pharmacy that next afternoon, I felt a growing sense of loyalty toward my new friend. I genuinely felt badly about the verbal battering he received each day at the hands of Lonnie and Scott, even though I was too timid to intervene.

"You know, those guys at school are just idiots. You know that, right?"

Aidan shrugged as we approached the front door of Metzger's Pharmacy. "They did the same thing in Omaha," he said calmly.

The bell rang above the door announcing our entrance into Metzger's Pharmacy. I had a hard time keeping up with Aidan as he sprinted to the back of the store.

Mr. Metzger was standing at the prescription dispensing counter in the back. He reminded me of a kindly mad scientist with his unruly grey hair, bright red bowtie and lab coat.

"Mr. Metzger! Can we play pinball?" Aidan's voice was breathless with excitement.

"It's all yours, kiddo," Mr. Metzger replied with a sweeping, showy gesture toward the pinball machine.

"And this is Matt!"

Mr. Metzger smiled and gave me a small salute. "Just keep it down to a low roar!" he called as we approached the pinball machine.

And there it was. I had never seen such an elaborate pinball machine. It had a circus theme and was called "Big Top Menagerie." Circus wagons, elephants, tigers, clowns and other circus accoutrements abounded in garish, flashing glory. Aidan pointed to an image of a circus carousel near the top of the machine. "If you get the ball into the slot at the center of the carousel, you can get literally millions of extra points. I've never been able to do it," Aidan explained, still breathless with excitement. "Now that there are two of us, I bet we can do it!"

Then I realized what Aidan meant. A plastic button on either side of the machine governed the movement of the flippers to propel the pinball. Aidan could operate one button with his right hand but the prosthetic hand was useless in manipulating the button on the opposite side of the machine. So I took my position operating the left-sided button and Aidan took the right-sided button. The first ball loaded promptly after Aidan fed the machine a quarter. Flashing lights and campy circus music followed. On that first outing, I learned to sync the activation of my flipper with Aidan's to propel the pinball. While we didn't hit the coveted carousel, we had a blast and earned triple bonus points several times.

And so began a new after-school routine. We would hit Metzger's with pockets heavy with quarters. Aidan would buy a foil packet of shredded bubble gum that resembled chewing tobacco. We would take huge pinches of bubble gum, our cheeks bulging as we navigated the pinball machine.

We also played a fair amount of basketball at my house. Aidan was absolutely the best HORSE player I've ever seen. He was amazingly accurate using only his right arm. He could use the prosthetic arm in combination with his right arm to set up the ball, but he chose to solely use his right arm. Most ten year-old kids had stick-like arms, but Aidan's right arm was quite muscular.

We also used to play a game we made up called "Ricochet." We would take a kickball and throw it as hard as we could against the garage door. (Good thing my dad didn't find out because he had just repainted that door the summer before!) The object was to see who could ricochet the ball farthest into the vacant lot across the street. The ultimate goal was to ricochet the ball into the woods bordering the far end of the lot. Aidan did this more than once. We even got poison ivy searching for the kickball in the woods on one occasion. I'll never forget Aidan's stance during a game of "Ricochet." He would bring his leg up like a baseball pitcher, wielding the ball in only his right arm, and then quickly hop out of the way as the ball ricocheted. I would throw the ball against the garage door using both hands with much poorer results. Several times I was hit by my own ricocheting ball because I couldn't get out of the way fast enough!

And forget about playing water balloons with this guy! Aidan and I would have marathon battles in the backyard. His powerful right arm packed quite a wallop. If Aidan hit you with a water balloon, it felt (and looked!) like a bee sting!

Over the next several months, our parents also became good friends. Aidan's mother Martha would walk over to pick him up from our home in the evening. More often than not, my mom would wave her in to stay for supper. She and Aidan became part of our family. I don't know when it started, but I began calling her Aunt Martha. It was getting difficult to remember back to when Aidan and his mom hadn't been a part of our lives.

School was still a minefield for Aidan. We were having lunch in the cafeteria. Our usual table by the window was occupied, so we took seats across from each other right off the main aisle from the serving line. Aidan's mom paid for Aidan to have hot lunches twice a week. Today was one of those days. Aidan was about to tuck into a giant platter of spaghetti when I saw them coming down the aisle.

Before I knew it, Lonnie had arrived at our table with Scott and Devon in tow. Devon stood behind Lonnie and Scott, looking nervously around and shifting from foot to foot. He was either not on board or a really good lookout in the event a teacher was watching us. Aidan watched calmly as Lonnie spat a big wad of saliva-coated chewing gum right into the middle of his platter of spaghetti.

"Oh, I'm sorry," Lonnie said with mock sincerity. "I thought this was the garbage can!"

Then they were off. My heart sank as Scott returned to top off Aidan's spaghetti with a balled-up gum wrapper.

Aidan took his fork and started probing the spaghetti. I could tell by the intent look on his face that he was trying to find a way to salvage his ruined meal if at all possible.

"Hey, Aidan," I said. "Let's split my lunch. Honest, my mom packs enough for three people." It was the truth. Today's peanut butter and jelly sandwich appeared to weigh about a pound. Mom had probably used at least half a jar of peanut butter. Aidan nodded and I started to subdivide the sandwich, but not before Lonnie returned to steal the only other item on Aidan's school lunch tray – a granola bar. I watched as Lonnie sneered and then threw the granola bar into the garbage, still wrapped.

Aidan remained calm as always. "Hey," he said through a massive mouthful of peanut butter.

"Hey what?"

"Today. Today's the day. We're not leaving Metzger's after school until we do it!"

I couldn't help but smile.

An empty package of shredded bubble gum and four empty bottles of blue Gatorade sat at our feet as we doggedly played pinball at Metzger's later that afternoon. Mr. Metzger laughed behind the counter after one particularly enthusiastic game that ended in "woo-hooing" after getting quadruple bonus points.

But Aidan was focused like a laser on the holy grail of the "Big Top Menagerie"- the fabled circus carousel. In the background, I could see Mr. Metzger closing the pharmacy for the evening. Then he strolled over to us and stood at Aidan's side of the pinball machine, hands in pockets and periodically glancing at his watch.

Then it happened. Two hours and twenty seven minutes after our arrival, I almost missed a flip. To be truthful, my wrists were just gassed at that point. That near miss made my heart skip a beat as Aidan was still sharply focused. We watched the pinball meander past the snarling tigers to rest in…

…the carousel! Synthetic calliope music began bellowing out of the pinball machine. All of the lights were flashing with an almost stroboscopic effect! The dings were barely a second apart as our points ramped up. We were screaming and jumping and high-fiving with abandon. Even Mr. Metzger joined in on a high-five. The pinball sat in the center of the carousel like a crown jewel. It was apparently not going anywhere soon. The cacophony of light, sound and music went on and on as we screamed ourselves into veritable exhaustion. Mr. Metzger looked at his watch again as the pinball machine continued to belch out sound and music. It wasn't lost on me that we were keeping him past closing time. Aidan was truly oblivious, his eyes locked on the carousel and the mounting point totals. Mr. Metzger actually started eyeing the power cord after about three minutes. I said a silent prayer that he wouldn't pull the plug on the machine in the interest of time. At the four minute mark, the action stopped and we found ourselves to be the highest scoring player (really players) ever on this machine! Ten minutes later, Mr. Metzger sent us on our way with a grandfatherly pat on the shoulder and two cold and complimentary Gatorades.

We began walking home. My house would come up first and Aidan's was another one and one half blocks due east. We were both late for dinner, but who cared? A dream had been reached after a very mediocre day at school!

I think Aidan saw them first because his hoarse laughter abruptly stopped. Lonnie and Scott were sitting on the curb. Devon stood in back of them, rocking nervously back and forth on his heels with his hands tucked into his hoodie.

Of course, Lonnie spoke first as we walked up. "What are you two girls up to tonight?" he sneered.

Aidan and I silently soldiered past them on the sidewalk to Lonnie and Scott's taunts of "Cyborg," "Freak" and "Freakshow!"

I was on such an adrenaline high from the pinball marathon that I suddenly felt fearless. I whirled around and yelled, "He had cancer, dumb asses! Don't you guys know anything?"

I heard Aidan suck in a breath as we kept walking. It felt good to defend him and I also felt a strange newfound confidence.

Then Lonnie shouted back, "Your mom must be a retard to have a freakshow kid like you!"

Aidan stopped walking. A strange and unfamiliar expression appeared on his face. At first, he looked confused – like being called on in class when you weren't listening at all. Then the look turned "dark" for lack of a better word. But my surprise and shock were just beginning as Aidan let out a wail. The intonation contour of it smacked of "Oh-no-I-don't-want-to-do-this-but-you're-going-to-make-me!"

Then something happened that I cannot unsee, even forty years later. With a bloodcurdling scream, Aidan violently tore off his prosthetic arm. I had never seen the stump just below his shoulder, but I could see it in the moonlight now. The skin on the stump had been torn in the process and blood was pouring indelicately from it.

Aidan wielded the prosthetic arm in his right hand like a club, "stump" side up, and began rapidly walking toward Lonnie, Scott and Devon. Scott immediately ran off and plunged into some bushes down the block. Lonnie was so startled as Aidan approached that he lost his footing and fell onto his back.

Aidan was still screaming as he raised the prosthetic arm in the air above Lonnie. Lonnie scooted backward on his hands and behind, resulting in Aidan's swing missing by about three inches. Aidan did not appear about to stop. The same laser intensity that he showed at the pinball machine appeared to be operating here. Aidan swung the prosthetic arm even higher, muscles rippling, on the next attempt. Lonnie reflexively turned on his side, again just missing the blow. At that point, I locked eyes with Devon who, as usual, was anxiously lingering in the background. I could swear that Devon gave me a small nod but I can't be completely sure.

Lonnie had managed to stand up now as Aidan readied another swing. The next part happened so incredibly quickly that there was no time to process it. Within a split second, Devon delivered a karate-style kick that landed just below Lonnie's chin. He spilled back onto the ground, this time on his stomach. Then Devon circled over and helped me defuse Aidan with surprising gentleness.

Lonnie was not hurt but uncharacteristically silent as we left the scene. Aidan was also uncharacteristically silent as we walked. But something else was different about him, too. At the time, I couldn't identify it but I know now that his spirit was broken.

"Dude, are you okay? You are like seriously bleeding." I noticed blood continuing to issue forth from the stump. His sleeveless basketball shirt was soaking with blood on one side.

"I'm fine," he whispered, still carrying his prosthetic arm like a truncheon. I watched him walk up the path to his front porch. I could see Aunt Martha take him indoors. The words "What happened to you?" floated out into the warm night air.

The following day, Aidan didn't come to school. Lonnie and Scott didn't appear to be in attendance either. I saw Devon once from a distance and he looked dejected.

I clock-watched in class the entire day. Six and a half hours could not go fast enough! Immediately after the bell, I literally ran out of the parking lot to Aidan's house.

Aunt Martha answered the door. She smiled sweetly at me. She looked desperately tired with half moon-shaped dark circles under her eyes. She said that Aidan required eight stitches last night in the ER, but that he was fine now and resting in bed.

"Can I see him?" My voice sounded timid and plaintive to me.

"No, honey. I'm afraid not today. His shoulder is really hurting him. But come by tomorrow," she replied, to my great disappointment.

As I walked away, Aunt Martha called my name. I whirled around, hoping she had changed her mind about visiting.

Instead: "Matt, thank you for sticking up for Aidan." And then: "Thank you for being such a good friend to my son." Then she closed the door.

Lonnie and Scott were both back at school the next day but they completely ignored me, to my vast relief. I went through the motions at school until the last bell. I then sprinted over to Aidan's house.

The house was quiet. All of the curtains were closed and the garage door was shut. I didn't see Aunt Martha's car anywhere. My only choice was to go home.

That night, I tried calling Aidan before bed. I would have been happy even just talking to Aunt Martha for an update, but it wasn't happening. The phone simply rang infinitely.

I couldn't sleep at all after that. At almost 11:00 PM, I went downstairs. My parents were still up. They were standing in the darkened hallway off the kitchen, location of our only telephone. My mom was talking to someone on the phone as my dad, still in his plumber's uniform, leaned tiredly against the wall. I stayed behind the corner so I could still hear but not make my presence known.

The caller was Aunt Martha. From what I could piece together, Aidan was in the hospital. I heard discussion on my mom's end of Aidan having a very high fever and something called "staph."

"What would you like us to tell Matt?" my mom asked Aunt Martha in hushed tones. "Okay. I see." She then concluded the call with love and good wishes.

Then my dad entered the conversation. "So what did she say, Carol?"

"It's serious, Pete. Aidan's temperature was still 103.5 last hour. He has a raging infection from tearing off the prosthesis so violently."

"Poor kiddo," my dad mused. "What do we tell Matt?"

"Martha wants to wait until tomorrow for us to tell Matt anything. She thinks he should be better by then."

At supper the next evening, I pushed my food to various locations around the plate, eventually rotating them back to the positions in which they were originally served. My appetite was non-existent. My dad offered to play HORSE with me after supper but I declined.

Later that same evening, I was attempting to do my increasing backlog of homework when the phone rang. This time I sat on the steps to eavesdrop. I knew it had to be Aunt Martha.

My mom started to cry after several seconds of listening to the caller. Aidan now had some strange thing called "sepsis" and was on some contraption called a "ventilator." He also had something called "minimal cortical function" based on tests completed earlier. Aunt Martha wondered if mom could come to the hospital to sit with her. Aidan would be removed from the ventilator in the morning.

My dad arrived in my room several minutes later. He sat down on my bed. I pretended to do homework at my desk as tears ran down my face onto the loose leaf pages.

"Matt, Aunt Martha called. Aidan's in the hospital. He isn't doing too well, kiddo. An infection got the better of him and he can't breathe without a machine right now. His brain is slowly shutting down, too. Okay, there, I've said it." I turned around to look at my dad. He was crying, too.

Neither of us could sleep, so my dad talked me into a half-hearted game of HORSE around midnight. Mom called from the hospital to tell us that Aidan would be taken off the ventilator at 6 AM for his trip to heaven.

At 4:30 AM, my dad and I sat in the backyard at our picnic table. He tried to interest me in a heaping bowl of ice cream, but I just couldn't do it. It was a beautiful, balmy, starlit pre-dawn. I listened to my dad slurping on his ice cream at the other end of the picnic table and looked up at the stars.

I thought of Aidan. What would things look like when he was taken off the ventilator, I wondered. I pictured a fish out of water, flapping around on a pier with eyes wide open, gills moving frantically. I decided that Aidan's eyes would probably not be wide open given that his brain was also dying.

I kept looking at the stars. The first pink fingers of dawn were beginning to creep in. First one star disappeared, then another. Then entire groups of stars winked out, replaced by a different sort of light.

My story was over. Colton's eyes never left mine but his blank expression remained unchanged. He was pale now, his ruddy cheeks gone.

"Okay," I sighed. "Do you have any questions?"

Colton silently shook his head.

"Okay, get out of here. I don't want to see you for a while." I put my head in my hands briefly and then stood up. Colton turned to leave and I looked down at the floor.

Then I heard Colton say timidly, "Dad?"

I looked up as Colton came over to me. I was in disbelief. He hadn't hugged me this long and hard since he was seven years old. I could feel his warm tears on my face.

After Colton left, I opened the blinds in my office to see starlight. Had my story taken that long? The sun had been shining brightly overhead when we began. I thought of how many times one type of light had replaced another since Aidan lived…the endless cycles of life and death, good and evil, cruelty and forgiveness.

HARDTACK

Alton, Mary and I started up the weedy path to the weathered barn. A 102 year-old woman had recently bequeathed the entire farm to the Minnesota Historical Society. It consisted of a Civil War-era farmhouse, corn crib and the barn we were approaching. The entire property consisted of about six acres and had been vacant for many decades.

The door creaked as if in protest as we entered the barn. We had been charged with inspecting the property to determine what steps needed to be taken to promote the development of a possible Civil War-era farm museum.

Alton started comically as a bird darted from the rafters.

"Too much coffee this morning, eh Alton?" Mary quipped.

I truly enjoyed my volunteer position with the historical society. While I had always enjoyed American history, the volunteerism performed an important personal function for me as well. I was reeling from an increasingly nasty divorce. At present, I had lost custody of my two children, ages eight and ten years. Studying and exploring the past was a comfort to me. It also afforded an escape from my long, mundane hours as an insurance adjuster in Minneapolis.

The barn had a well-compacted dirt floor and several stalls for horses and livestock. A rickety ladder led to the hayloft. None of us trusted the ladder enough to climb up, but the loft appeared to be empty. The main floor of the barn appeared equally vacant except for a solitary rusty milk bucket.

But then I saw it. In a darkened corner, an ancient burlap sack came into view.

"Alton, Mary!" I waved my fellow volunteers over.

I bent down on one knee and put on my work gloves.

"Be careful touching it, Kevin," Mary cautioned. "It's probably going to fall apart."

I nodded. My hand reached out timidly as my heart thudded in my chest with anticipation. A cloud of brackish dust came up as my hand lightly contacted the burlap. As slowly as my excitement would permit, I opened the bag.

Alton was crouching down beside me now as the contents of the bag came into full view.

"Well, I'll be!" Alton exclaimed.

The bag was almost completely full of what resembled crackers.

"It's hardtack!" Mary added. I had only read about the rock-solid biscuits that were used to sustain soldiers and sea farers in the 17th, 18th and 19th centuries. Hardtack was virtually bulletproof and could only be consumed by dunking it in coffee or boiling it to soften it.

Cautiously, I withdrew a piece of hardtack. As advertised, it felt like stone.

"What you're holding is probably more than 150 years old," Alton remarked.

I was stunned into silence as I pictured a Civil War soldier reaching into his pack for a piece, hunger raging.

We completed our tour and notes on the property. As we walked back to our cars, I patted what felt incredibly like a hockey puck in my jacket pocket. Each of us was taking a piece of hardtack home.

I lived in a three bedroom condo in downtown Minneapolis. The first level featured a large, octagonal-shaped kitchen with a small family room. The master bedroom and ensuite were off the kitchen. The downstairs area contained the remaining two bedrooms, a full bath and a large sitting area. This part of the condo depressed me the most. As I walked downstairs, I had so many times pictured my two children doing homework or watching TV down here. I imagined rousing them for school to their reluctant groans. Sadly, my wife's attorney (AKA "hatchet man") had waged a bitter and cunning court battle that resulted in my loss of custody. I was currently appealing for "crumbs," i.e. one weekend a month visitation, but there had been radio silence from my attorney lately. And the battle royal was getting very expensive.

I stood in the darkness, peering into the empty bedrooms that would hopefully contain my son and daughter one weekend a month. I sat on the floor, suddenly feeling exhausted from the fight and financial pressures. I needed more income, but I didn't want to necessarily take a second job. My volunteer position with the historical society would be the first thing to go and I needed it. I decided that the answer was right in front of me. I would rent out the two bedrooms. Tenants would have the entire lower level to themselves and we could share the kitchen. I stood up, feeling my knees creak. This was it! I bounded up the stairs for a shower and to write an ad.

I sat on the side of my bed, laptop balancing on my thighs. I smiled, glancing at the piece of hardtack on my nightstand. Then I began to compose an ad to post on-line:

RENTERS WANTED
CONDO IN METRO MINNEAPOLIS
SHARED KITCHEN
CLOSE TO EVERYTHING!
e-mail for details:
KevinD@spark.com

I was surprised to hear from a prospective renter less than a day later! He wanted to see it immediately. His name was Billy and he was from Ocala, Florida. He appeared to be about 30 years old with spiky black hair and a lean, rangy build. He laughed easily and had a smile that revealed every tooth. He seemed as relaxed as his southern drawl. He was single and worked as a third shift supervisor at an IT call center just outside of downtown.

"I really like it," he said, smiling hugely and running his hand lazily through his spiky black hair.

"Is the shared kitchen okay with you?" I asked.

"Sure. I work at night, so I don't think we'll collide too much in the kitchen." He chuckled.

"You know there will eventually be another tenant in the other bedroom."

"No problem. It'll be like living in the dorm at college again!" He laughed again but then a shadow crossed his face. "Aw, Mr. Duncan, I didn't mean to infer I'm a partier 'cause I'm not. Straight arrow here!"

"Yeah, I got you," I replied, unconcerned. "So you'll take it?"

"Yep!"

"All right! Welcome, Billy! Let's go upstairs and knock off some paperwork!"

Two days after Billy moved in, my second renter snapped up the remaining bedroom. Her name was Olive and she worked nights as an RN at Children's Hospital. She was somewhat shy but projected warmth in her few words. She was from Atlanta and also had a huge southern drawl.

I introduced Olive to Billy.

Billy laughed and flashed every tooth. "Imagine that! Two vampires for renters!"

I gave him a baffled look.

"I mean third shift workers!" he clarified.

"And two southerners!" I added.

Billy smiled at Olive but was completely silent.

"I do declare!" Olive finally said, never taking her eyes off Billy.

"Yee-haw!" crowed Billy, jumping into the air.

We all laughed.

The arrangement was perfect. I would have relative solitude and quiet given our differing work schedules. It would almost be like living alone but with an extra $1800 a month coming in. I decided to open up a separate bank account for just my rental proceeds. This would be my war chest for the ongoing divorce and custody proceedings. Leftover funds could be used to spoil the kids.

The condo life settled into a rhythm for the three of us very quickly. Billy worked from 11:30 PM to 8:00 AM and Olive worked 11:00 PM to 7:30 AM. Some days I barely saw or heard either of them. I worked from 9:30 AM to 6:00 PM. In some ways, I was right – it was a bit like living alone with extra income! I silently congratulated myself on this simple but apparently brilliant plan.

One morning, I awoke to hear Billy and Olive talking quietly in the kitchen. I was still getting used to sleeping with my door closed because the master led directly into the kitchen. I became very still and found myself eavesdropping. The voices were unmistakably theirs but the conversation was markedly strange.

"Brother Giles, the pork is getting rancid and we haven't much more," pleaded the voice that was Olive's. "We only have a single potato left and that is full of weevils!"

A pause ensued.

Then the voice that was Billy hissed, "Sister Julia, put salt to the pork and cut out the weevils! These damn Yankees are going to starve us to death!"

"Brother, we also need more wood for the fire!"

"Sister, it's always more you need!" rasped Billy in a frustrated tone.

I felt disoriented hearing this but even more so when the foul odor of rancid food being boiled emanated into my bedroom.

That did it. I had to see what was going on. I pulled on a bathrobe and ran my fingers through my sleep-tossed hair. I closed my eyes briefly before opening the door to enter the kitchen to see…

Olive and Billy were sitting at the kitchen table sharing a large pizza. Music was playing softly on Billy's phone and they were both laughing quietly.

"Well, mornin' Kevin!" Billy crowed enthusiastically. "Hope we didn't wake you!"

"No, no," I said, still dumbfounded at the discrepancy between what I had just heard and what I was now seeing. "I've got to get up for work anyway." Still shocked, I rummaged through the cupboard for a coffee mug.

Without standing, Billy pulled out the empty chair next to him. "Join us for some pizza, Kev?"

I swallowed. Pizza looked revolting to me early in the morning but I found I couldn't think clearly for now. Before I knew it, I was having a slice and hearing about both of their nights at work.

During a brief lull in the conversation, I found myself saying, "I'm sorry!"

"For what?" Olive's expression was one of a nurse's concern.

"It's just…I thought I heard you two talking about rotten pork and potatoes when I was in bed. Absurd, right?"

Billy had a mouthful of pizza and his eyes remained locked on Olive. "I'm sorry, what?" he finally managed.

"I heard something about cutting weevils out of a potato because it was the last one you had!" I knew I sounded certifiable but I needed clarification desperately.

Billy then let loose his trademark toothy laugh and slapped his thigh. "What're you smokin' back there, Kevin? You gotta get me some, too!" He was in hysterics now.

"Maybe I was dreaming, but I could smell something weird, too," I continued.

"More pizza, anybody? Otherwise I'm clearing the table." Olive was on her feet and out of the conversation.

The next two days passed contentedly without much further interaction with Billy or Olive other than brief greetings. My puzzlement at what happened that morning gradually subsided until the following Friday. I woke to hear footsteps in the kitchen.

"We got one!" said Billy.

"What?" countered Olive.

"Sister, must I explain everything? A Union soldier!"

"When?"

"Last evening. Don't worry. I gave him a good beating and bound him up in the corn crib."

"Brother Giles, you musn't do this! You must let him go at once!"

"Let him go? No! Besides, I can't. I broke his legs."

"Brother, this is an abomination-"

Olive (or Julia) stopped there because I abruptly flung the door open and entered the kitchen.

Billy and Olive were seated at the kitchen table, each with a takeout coffee and silently scrolling through their phones.

"Kevin, good mornin'!" Billy looked up from his phone. "You forget something?"

I realized that I was only in my underwear in my haste to enter the kitchen. "What's going on here, guys?"

Billy shrugged as his genial smile faded. Olive was silent.

"Are you guys rehearsing for a play or something?"

Olive's eyes grew large and she slowly shook her head. Billy was uncharacteristically silent and serious but then he said, "Are you okay, Kevin? Come sit. Sorry I didn't think to bring you a coffee."

My temper was building like wildfire. "Cut the crap!" I hissed. "We're not talking about coffee."

"Then what do you want to talk about?" Billy said carefully, his arm lazily draped over the remaining empty kitchen chair. "You have something to say, just go on and say it."

Olive's expression had escalated to fearfulness at this point.

"Are you two related?"

Billy laughed but quickly suppressed it. "No. We just met when we signed on with you!"

My fists were balled at my sides. My eyes moved silently from one to the other but I had no further words at that point. I left the kitchen and showered for work.

That night, in the quiet of the empty condo, I lay sleepless. In the moonlight, I could see the piece of hardtack still on the nightstand. Was I hallucinating or having some sort of emotional breakdown? The last two years had certainly not been easy for me. Maybe I needed a vacation. The thought of leaving Olive and Billy alone in the condo for a week felt sinister to me. Another possibility occurred to me. What if Billy really was holding and torturing someone? Wouldn't it be my duty to report it? I reached over the piece of hardtack to retrieve my cell phone. I could dial 911 or talk to the police department, but what would I credibly tell them? The conversation between Olive and Billy (or was it Julia and Giles) was veiled, menacing and antiquated, but I could not prove anything.

I put the phone down and held the piece of hardtack in my hand, cool and firm as stone. I thought of how durable this small biscuit had been down through the centuries. Too bad I wasn't that durable, I thought.

In the wee hours, my sleeplessness morphed into a plan. I knew what I had to do. Tomorrow night I would follow Billy when he left the house for work. If someone was really in danger, I would then have proof.

I set a vibrating alarm on my phone for 11:00 PM so I could have a "cat nap" before following Billy tonight. I heard the refrigerator door open and close. Then I heard footsteps on the stairs outside. I crawled furtively to my bedroom window that faced the parking lot. I watched as Billy placed something in a garbage can and then entered his car.

I had earlier parked in the other lot on the opposite side of the condo development to make my presence more furtive.

I followed Billy's Jeep Wrangler from about four car lengths distance. I was pleased that there was more traffic on the road than I had expected at this late hour, thus providing better camouflage for my surveillance.

Billy exited the expressway about three miles out of downtown. He turned right and proceeded to drive into a strip mall. The strip mall was in complete darkness except for the far south end. The sign read "IT Solutions," the call center at which Billy worked. He parked directly in front of the brightly lit cubiculed office space. I carefully parked between two other cars at the opposite end of the parking lot. I watched as Billy slid a messenger bag over his shoulder and proceeded into work. His hand was on the front door and then he stopped. I held my breath, slinking deeper into my car seat and continuing to monitor the rear view mirror.

To my horror, Billy began striding rapidly and resolutely to my car. He crouched down and pounded on the driver's side window. I was completely trapped. I rolled down the window.

"Hey, Billy!" I began.

Billy was biting his lip in either anger or confusion or a bit of both.

"Kevin! What're you doing here, bro?"

"I…" My brain spun for an answer. "I was looking for a bite." My intonation lilted slightly like a question.

"Oh," said Billy. "Well, then you need to get back on the breezeway for another two exits. There's an all-night diner and a Taco Bell there. This is pretty much just the land of the industrial park!" He laughed, his teeth gleaming under the sodium vapor light.

"Oh," I said, already turning the key in the ignition.

"Oh! And Kevin!"

I looked up at Billy.

"It's late. Be careful out here," he added before turning to leave.

Another sleepless night ensued, partially because I felt terminally embarrassed about our encounter. However, I was glad that Billy was really at work versus torturing a kidnapped victim with broken legs. I fell into a fitful sleep.

Bright sun then poured into the bedroom. The voices in the kitchen began.

"Brother Giles, I beg of you. Let this poor man go!"

"Let him go? LET HIM GO? The only thing I will let this bastard Yankee do is DIE!"

"Brother, killing one soldier will not win the war."

A short silence followed. "Sister Julia, your country is the South! You ingrate! I will kill him this very night!"

Olive/Julia was sobbing now. "I beg of you, Giles," she said in a broken voice. "Have mercy."

"Mercy? What is mercy until the South rises again?!" Billy/Giles raged. He appeared to be devolving in his anger. "I will cut out his eyes first and then peel away his northern skin!"

"Have mercy, please!" Olive/Julia wailed.

I sat up on the edge of the bed, shaking and paralyzed. Then I saw it. The piece of hardtack was glowing like the fires of hell.

That evening, I requested a meeting in the kitchen with both Billy and Olive before they left for work. We sat at the kitchen table.

"Okay, here it is," I said. "This arrangement is just not working out. I am ending the lease, effective on the first of the month. If you need help packing up or moving, I am willing to assist. Any questions?"

"Why?" said Billy, shrugging and clearly blindsided.

"I…I don't want to get into it. It just isn't working out."

"We like it here," piped in Olive. "It's very convenient to my work and-"

Billy interrupted. "Did y'all find someone who can pay a higher rent?"

"No, I just want to end our arrangement. You're fine." I almost winced at the lie.

Billy stood over me. "Does this have anything to do with you following me the other night?" He whistled through his teeth with apparent disgust. "Paranoid much?" he added, leaving the room.

The next morning, Billy came silently into the kitchen as I sipped coffee at the table. Billy's sunny Ocala smile had been replaced by a scowl.

"Keys," he whispered, placing two sets on the table. "Olive's already gone."

I nodded and pocketed the keys. "Good luck, Billy," I replied.

He held my gaze for a moment. Then he hissed, "You Yankees are all the same." He shook his head in visible disgust and left.

SPRINGTIME

My mother and I were alone in the infusion suite. It was her last scheduled chemotherapy session. I looked around the humble room, thinking of all the hours we had spent here together as my mother fought the ovarian cancer that would likely soon claim her life. Sometimes we giggled about old family memories. Sometimes we watched movies. Other times I simply and silently held her hand as she slept.

The nurse came in briefly to check on the progress of the infusion. When he left, the conversation began.

"I'm going to be gone soon," said my mother. I hung my head, thinking of her oncologist's words at the last appointment – "response not what we hoped…"

My mother went on. "Jean, you're not just my daughter. You are my best friend in the whole world."

I took in my mother's ravaged features. Her reddened eyes were rimmed with tears. I gently rubbed her bruised arm.

"So, when I pass, you and I will need a way to communicate if you need anything. It's not like we'll be able to call or text one another."

I nodded silently.

My mother straightened slightly in the infusion chair. "I know!" she said, her expression brightening. "How about we choose a word – like a code word. If you're in trouble and need my help, just think of or say that word. Then I can work with God to focus on your situation."

I finally spoke. "How will I know that you heard me?"

My mother put a finger to her lips in thought. "Someone else will say the word in your company."

"This sounds crazy."

"It's not. Consider it part of making my final arrangements. I have to keep you safe. I don't stop being your mother when I die. Life is hard, Jean."

How right she was. Two weeks before my mother's ovarian cancer diagnosis, my husband requested a divorce, seemingly out of the blue.

"Jean, are you on board?"

"Sure, mom."

"Now, what should the word be?"

I was at a loss.

My mother continued. "We don't want it to be a super common word or false alarms will be constantly going off..."

I laughed. "Yeah, imagine if we picked 'the' or 'and'!"

My mother pursed her lips in thought. "I've got it!" she exclaimed, grabbing my hand. "The word will be SPRINGTIME."

To say I was lonely in the initial weeks after my mother's death was a bleak understatement. COVID-19 had now hit and I was spending most of my time alone in my one bedroom apartment in Winnetka. My job as a librarian was on hold because the library was closed given the public health situation.

I was so incredibly tired of the Internet but boredom drove me back there again and again. I opened my laptop at the kitchen table and logged onto Facebook. Against my better judgment, I typed "Brian Henderson" in the search box. This was my ex-husband who almost wordlessly left our marriage last year.

The page loaded devoid of privacy settings. That was classic Brian – outgoing to a "t" and always wanting the world to know what he was doing. As a quiet librarian, I was apparently not enough for him.

And there it was. A photo of Brian with the Navy Pier ferris wheel in the background, cheeks rosy from the cold and his arm around a petite brunette woman. The photo was captioned with "Don't let the cold keep you at home. We didn't! Jenn and I had a wonderful Saturday. Now home for a fire and hot chocolate!"

I slammed the laptop shut, a fearful lump rising in my throat. I was nearly choking as I reached for my cell phone to call my oldest friend Lena. She lived in Schiller Park with her husband Mark and their six children. Lena always had time for me and Mark had a penchant for entertaining children so I had no hesitation in calling her.

Lena arrived at my apartment that afternoon. As she wriggled out of her jacket, she said, "Eew, I just found another Cheerio sticking in my hair. These kids are going to be the death of me."

We sat down on the sofa.

Lena continued. "I would have been here sooner, kiddo, but the dog barfed all over the kitchen floor on my way out. Then Jody, my little guy, joined the party with more barfing. Anyway, I left Mark in a sea of vomit."

I silently handed the laptop to Lena, Brian's Facebook page still loaded.

Lena's eyes turned from humorous mock disgust with her story to genuinely downcast.

"Aw, honey. This is so hard," she said, hugging me.

My tears were falling in rapid, silent streams. "This is so ridiculous. I'm not a teenager anymore. I'm 37 years old!"

"But he was yours at one time," soothed Lena.

"People move on. That's life. Why am I so sad about this?" I was starting to feel very short of breath. My chest tightened. Was I having a panic attack?

"Honey, listen. Grief is normal in a situation like this. 'We wouldn't grieve if we didn't love.' I think Queen Elizabeth said that."

I was now very short of breath.

Lena continued. "We must make a pact. No social media for a while. No Facebook, Twitter, Instagram or the like. It's not mentally healthy for you. Capiche?"

I was now on my feet, gasping for air.

"Jean, are you okay?" Lena bounded up from the sofa.

"I – I think I'm having an anxiety attack. I'm going to the bathroom to splash some water on my face."

"Want me to come with?"

"No, wait here. I'll be right back."

I stumble-stepped down the narrow hallway to the bathroom. When I turned on the light, my face looked positively ashen with purple crescents under my eyes. I gagged, feeling a wave of nausea. I coughed.

When I opened my eyes, Lena was in the bathroom with me. My hands, face and the mirror were sprayed with blood.

Lena was a huge help in the days after I was released from the hospital. She brought over meals and kept me company. She said Mark was "managing" with the kids.

I had been diagnosed with a very rare form of lung cancer. The one year survival rate was less than 25% and the five year survival rate was less than 5%. My doctor at Northwestern University Hospital recommended concurrent radiation and chemotherapy. I thought of the endless hours in the infusion room with my mother at Rush, to no avail.

"Can I do nothing?" I asked Dr. Evans.

He paused. "Yes. Hospice care is always an option."

Lena had driven me to that appointment and was visibly upset when I recounted the conversation on the way home.

"You have to fight! You just have to!" she cried.

I was already tired. I leaned my head against the car window and started whispering the word "springtime" over and over again.

It was still dark outside when I heard pounding on my front door. Startled, I pulled on my robe and peered through the peep hole. It was Lena, hair askew, her hands full of various papers.

"What time is it? What're you doing here?"

"The time is NOW!" Lena said excitedly. She led me to the kitchen table and turned on the overhead light.

"I've been up all night!" she opened.

"It's still night," I yawned, noting the time at 4:37 AM.

Lena plopped a stack of computer print-outs in front of me. "Jean, I found a researcher in Houston who's doing a clinical trial on your type of lung cancer!" Lena riffled through the stack of print-outs in manic fashion. "Her name is Dr. Alison McVeigh, Chair of General Oncology at MD Anderson on the University of Texas Medical Center campus."

I yawned again. "Yeah, I've heard of MD Anderson."

"So," Lena said, pointing to a statistical table on the print-out. "She is documenting one year survival rates of 78% and five year survival rates of 69%. Her regimen involves chemoradiation and a drug called…" She riffled through the stack for another print-out. "It's a drug called Ameliova."

Lena kneeled on the floor and grabbed me by both shoulders. "Will you go?"

"Go?"

"Yes, go to see Dr. McVeigh?"

I swallowed, still waking up. "Okay, sure."

"Great! I'll go with you. Let's call her office this morning and then I can work on getting our flight."

"What about Mark and the kids?"

"This is payback for all of the hard time in pregnancy and labor," Lena winked. "Men escape all of that!"

By 10:30 that morning, we had secured an appointment with Dr. McVeigh for next week Thursday. Our flight was on Wednesday. I was surprised at how quickly things were coming together. Maybe the tide was turning.

I kept whispering the word "springtime" like a mantra.

The phone rang late at night on that Sunday. It was Lena. She and Mark along with one of the kids had COVID.

"I'm so sorry," she practically wailed over the phone. "We're all in quarantine. We think Jody's teacher had COVID, too. What a mess!"

"Are you feeling okay?"

"Fine except for sniffles. I'm so, so sorry about this, Jean."

I checked into my spacious room at the hotel attached to MD Anderson Cancer Center. I wouldn't even have to venture outside for my appointment with Dr. McVeigh, although the temperature in Houston was a pleasant 65 degrees. It would be nice to sit outside on the campus in shirt sleeves instead of the blustery 20 degree weather in Chicagoland.

The evening before my appointment, I ventured downstairs to the hotel lobby for a stroll. I noticed a library room. A huge leather sofa and grand piano dominated the room. A young woman was playing Chopin's Nocturne on the piano. She smiled gently at me, her bald head catching the soft light. I sat down on the sofa as I enjoyed this concert for one.

Dr. McVeigh was a grandmotherly woman with a shiny grey bob. She reviewed my medical history and records from Dr. Evans. She sat on a small stool with coasters, expertly navigating it back and forth from me to her desktop computer. I was relieved to hear that I was, in her words, a "stellar candidate" for a clinical trial with Ameliova and chemoradiation. Per Dr. McVeigh, there was no time like the present and treatment would commence immediately. She had only one caveat.

"Jean, you realize that my survival rates are not 100%. This is not a miracle cure."

I nodded, having no illusions.

She went on to describe how all care and medication would be free for the clinical trial and that I would receive a generous stipend for food and lodging. This was a godsend because I was financially tapped out.

Dr. McVeigh was turned toward her computer as she said, "Hopefully by springtime this will all be behind you."

My heart leaped in my chest. "I'm sorry, when did you say?"

Dr. McVeigh turned and faced me. She appeared to think for a moment, locating her exact words. Then she looked me directly in the eye and said, "Springtime."

It was five years later on a steamy August morning. I was so short of breath I bent at the waist and briefly put my head between my legs. I felt my blood moving as my perspiration pinged onto the ground in droplets like rain.

But I recovered my breath very quickly. I was now a conditioned athlete. I had just completed a pre-dawn run of ten miles.

My next marathon was in springtime.

THE RETURN

It was over. Just like that.

I sat in the fading light in stunned stillness. My husband of twelve years, Evan, had passed away earlier that day during a business lunch with his regional manager. Andrew tearfully told me, "One minute, he's laughing and cutting up tomatoes from the salad bar on his plate. The next minute, he's clawing and grabbing at his throat and rolling around on the ground, fighting to breathe." Cardiopulmonary arrest followed and Evan passed away at Christ Hospital at 12:47 PM, despite heroic resuscitation efforts. He was 36 years old.

The doctor's impression was anaphylactic shock.

According to Jewish custom, Evan was buried almost immediately and he was not embalmed. I opted for a "green" burial in a biodegradable casket without a vault.

It was over. Just like that.

After the graveside portion of the funeral service concluded, I walked with Rabbi Stineman in the frigid air.

"I didn't even get to say goodbye to him," I lamented.

The rabbi stopped walking and regarded me. "Rebekah, try the following exercise at home. Find your favorite chair or most comfortable spot on the couch. Then close your eyes and talk to Evan. Let your feelings come forth naturally. Sometimes writing to the deceased can help, too."

"Thank you, Rabbi Stineman," I replied, knowing that this wouldn't work.

I desperately wanted to be alone in our home, despite Jewish custom. Evan and I had no immediate blood family, so our co-workers filled that role throughout our marriage. My teaching colleagues from Lakeview Elementary School and several of Evan's colleagues from Patrick Pharmaceuticals promised to stay in close touch.

Then I walked home from the cemetery. We lived in a mid-century ranch right across the street.

We used to joke that we would be "permanent residents" of the neighborhood.

That first night, I lay in bed pondering our last moments together. I was having breakfast at the kitchen table as Evan chased a pesky fly with the fly swatter flailing in his hand. I couldn't help but laugh as Evan unsuccessfully chased the fly wildly around the kitchen, his tie flying over his shoulder. A string of expletives accompanied each failed attempt to obliterate the fly.

"Language, young man!" I said in my best mock-stern schoolmarm's voice.

Now that same fly was circulating endlessly in the dark of our bedroom.

I slept fitfully, sometimes waking up to bat the fly away from my head. The clock read 3:17 AM. Then I heard it. It was a scuffling, scratching sound coming from what seemed to be the outside of our front door. I swear I heard the screen door rattling slightly as well. I froze. Could it be the wind blowing leaves up onto the front porch? Could it be an animal? Evan and I had both noticed more squirrels in our yard than usual this past fall. Normally, I would have implored

Evan to check on the situation. As I pulled on my bathrobe, I realized the courage I would need as a widow in matters both large and small.

Moonlight slanted into the quiet living room as I approached the front door. I tiptoed and looked out of the peephole. At that level, I saw nothing. I realized I would have to actually open the door to see what was causing the scuffling noise that was becoming more insistent by the second. I closed my eyes and swallowed. Then, like ripping a bandage off to minimize the pain, I flung open the front door.

A shadowy form lay in a heap at my front door, arms and legs splayed out haphazardly. It was clearly a human being. Could it be a homeless person seeking help or a drunk getting the wrong house at bar time? I turned on the porch light but then quickly turned it off when I realized who it was.

Evan!

Before I knew it, he was staggering in the front door. He seemed to have absolutely no equilibrium, his arms pin wheeling crazily in the moonlight. He crashed into the kitchen, knocking over two chairs and landing on top of the kitchen table with such force that one of the legs broke off. Then he smashed into the refrigerator backwards, sliding down the door and leaving a trail of mud. He was then sitting on the kitchen floor, legs splayed in front of him, moaning like a wounded animal.

I was rooted to my spot about ten feet away from him. Evan's hair and face were caked in dirt. His dark blue suit was torn and running with wet mud. His tie and dress shirt (given new, still in plastic, to the funeral director) were twisted and blackened with earth. I realized that I had my hand clamped tightly over my mouth in an effort not to scream. Somehow I knew that my panic and fear would not help Evan. I knew instinctively that he was more afraid than I.

I slowly approached Evan, then realizing that he had no pants on, only underwear. This made sense because Evan was only very briefly viewed in the casket from the waist up. His mud-caked legs were quaking. Hypothermia then became a concern of mine.

I crouched down and Evan began to scream in a muffled manner.

I turned on the kitchen light and calmly returned to him. He was pulling at his lips. Why couldn't he open his mouth? In horror, I could see blood trickling at the corners of his mouth. It dawned on me that the funeral director had likely sutured his mouth shut to prevent it from opening during visitation.

"Evan, I'll be right back," I said as calmly as I could over his escalating screams. I thundered into the bathroom and located a small pair of scissors in the first aid kit. Then I embarked on the surreal task of gently cutting the mouth sutures. When I completed my grisly task, the screaming only became louder. Evan bounded up and crashed over to the kitchen sink. To my horror, he pulled out several discolored clumps of a cotton-type material from his mouth. He faced me, panting, with sutures still dangling from his lips. Then he proceeded to vomit in projectile fashion over the entire kitchen.

Evan finally managed to stumble into our bedroom, pinballing from wall to wall. I was able to extricate him from the filthy suit jacket. I covered him up with several blankets as he shivered spasmodically. He was still awake and looking at me when he said his first words, "I'm home."

The next day passed surreally. Evan was begging for water but after several sips, he vomited intensively, soaking the bed and one of the bedroom walls. Later on, I offered him a cup of chicken broth that he accepted eagerly but with the same odiferous rejection by his stomach. "How could someone vomit so much when consuming so little?" I wondered during one of my many clean-up efforts. The doorbell and my cell phone rang multiple times that day but I didn't answer. The stench was almost unbearable but I soldiered on to care for the person I loved most in the world.

That evening, Evan became very congested. His almost constant cough was productive of tan-green phlegm. I was horrified to see dead earthworms in some of the phlegm. I took his temperature and it topped out at 103.2.

Evan was now apparently too weak to get out of bed and prodigiously incontinent. I did not have any adult undergarments on hand, nor could I leave the house to get them given Evan's worsening condition. So I improvised, swaddling him in extra sheets and fashioning a bedpan out of a cut-down piece of Tupperware.

"Evan, honey, I think we need to get you to a hospital!" I finally said. I held his hand, noticing the bruises, cuts, blood blisters, broken fingernails and even missing fingernails that were a testimony to his escape. His hand felt almost like a mitt it was so edematous.

Evan's intensely bloodshot eyes were running with pus but I could still see the panic in them. "No!" he cried hoarsely. "No hospital! How do we explain all of this?" The remaining loose sutures flapped at his lips as he spoke.

I bit my lip. I stroked his still dirt-caked hair. "Okay, Evan. No hospital."

"Just you!"

"Okay, just me."

By the next night, Evan was moaning almost constantly, albeit softly. I tried everything I could to soothe him. I was trying to give him a sponge bath by candlelight. I was also combing dirt out of his hair. The window was cracked but the stench was still surreal. I hummed lightly as I gently stroked the washcloth down Evan's arm.

He looked at me tenderly.

"Becky?"

I smiled at him.

Evan was beginning to cry. "I'm so sorry about all of this. I wrecked the whole house."

"Oh, Evan, no you didn't."

He paused. "I just wanted to come home."

I nodded. "I know. I love you, Evan."

"I love you more, Becky." He paused again. "Becky?"

"Yes, Evan?"

"I want you to know," he choked, tears streaming down his face. "I want you to know…"

"It's okay, honey. What?"

"I want you to know that I'm not some sort of zombie. I don't think I ever really died. I just woke up in there and…"

"Ssh, Evan," I soothed. "I know you're alive. Try to rest now."

"And Becky? At least this time I get to say goodbye. I felt so bad that I didn't get to say it the first time." Then he closed his eyes.

While Evan was sleeping, I contemplated the true terror of being buried alive. There were certainly anecdotal examples of this, particularly in antiquity when modern methods of verifying death did not exist. I remembered reading about a woman who had been mistakenly pronounced dead when in fact she was in a deep coma with undetectable vital signs. Fortunately, she "came to" prior to burial and was not embalmed. Embalming was the deal-breaker – no one survived that. I realized that Evan's return had the "perfect storm" quality to it – no embalming with quick burial per Jewish custom, biodegradable casket with no vault encasing it…

And proximity. Superhuman task of exiting the grave aside, he only had to make it across the street to return to me.

During my reverie, I failed to notice that Evan's breathing patterns had changed. He sounded like he was drowning from the inside out. He was no longer conscious or coughing. His breaths were now about ten seconds apart. Then I witnessed the last one –

-just as pounding ensued at the front door. Sobbing and startled, I couldn't take my eyes away from Evan. But then a man's voice thundered at the front door. "Rebekah Dartman, please open up. Riverdale Police Department! This is a welfare check!"

I covered my ears. I felt the urgency of responding to the door but my feet remained rooted next to Evan.

The pounding continued more insistently. The male voice now had an audibly irritated tone: "Rebekah Dartman, please open this door. This is the Riverdale Police. This is your last opportunity or we will be coming in!"

My steps felt dreamlike as I walked toward the front door. I actually had a profound thought as I opened the door: Most people suffer, die and are buried.

Evan was buried, suffered and died.

On the front porch were three policemen, two in riot or tactical gear. Apparently I answered in a nick of time because one of the officers had a battering ram aimed at the door.

The next few moments felt as surreal as everything else that had occurred over the past few days. I was quickly ushered into the family room and told not to move. I could see the slowly unfolding disgust and horror on the faces of the officers as they took in the ruined house and stench. I could hear one of the officers vomiting in the kitchen.

Several minutes later as police radios crackled, I was told to undress and change into what looked like a hazmat suit. I was also told that I was being detained for questioning and for my own safety. Later that evening, my detainment converted to an arrest.

The charges against me were mind-boggling and seemed to take forever to articulate aloud in court: vandalism, grave-robbing, tampering with a corpse...yada, yada, yada.

I went to trial with the only attorney I could properly afford, just one year out of school. The shrewd and cunning prosecutor ran roughshod over our shocked countenances. In particular, the prosecutor confused and discredited our star and expert witness, the aging medical examiner. This conniving and monstrous prosecutor found ways to cast doubt on all aspects of the medical examiner's befuddled testimony, including the fact that Evan's core body temperature and lack of decomposition were not compatible with being dead and buried, even for the short period that Evan was interred. Scads of DNA proof of life coated our bed, walls and floors but were glossed over in shocking fashion. My simple defense of caring for my dying husband as anyone would was largely ignored.

In the end, I was convicted on all charges and sentenced to fifteen months in state prison.

It was over. Just like that.

My attorney visited me in prison two months later to inform me that Evan's body had been embalmed and buried in a vault at an undisclosed location.

I served every bit of my fifteen month sentence but my release finally arrived on a grey November morning. My conditions included a six-month stay in a halfway house during which I would obtain gainful employment, followed by an additional eighteen months of closely supervised probation. I was not to visit any cemetery for any reason (excepting my own demise).

My parole officer Trudy stopped the car at the curb in front of the halfway house. It was a large, dreary bungalow at the top of a hill.

"Nervous?" Trudy smiled at me.

"Yes, very," I quickly replied, contemplating my first moments away from a cell in well over a year.

"That's normal," Trudy said. She gestured to the concrete staircase leading up to the bungalow. "Why don't you go up and ring the bell. I'm going to find a legal parking space and I'll join you."

I exited the car and swung my backpack over my shoulder and began to ascend the steps. When I reached the top, I rang the doorbell. While I was waiting for a response, I turned around to behold my new surroundings. From the hilltop porch of the bungalow, I could see a park with a crumbling tennis court and two kids playing basketball at a solitary rusty hoop with no net. I saw two church steeples and a factory with a smokestack in the distance. Otherwise it appeared to be a quiet residential area.

There were no cemeteries in sight.

WAGE WARRIORS

Things got really interesting the day my brother Bryce joined the Wage Warriors. Growing up, I had never known him to care about anything – only playing on the X-Box, keeping me out of his room and sleeping until 3 PM on the weekends. His hair was never combed and perpetually pushed up in the back like a rooster comb from couch slouching marathons. He always seemed to wear the same three to four well worn t-shirts. After high school, he started working full-time at the local Pizza Shack. I was still in high school, living with mom and Bryce just outside of Pittsburgh. Mom was a nurse at a nearby nursing home and always seemed tired and distracted – a victim of constantly changing shifts.

One night at a rare family dinner, Bryce took a cell phone from his pocket and absently put it on the table.

"Where did you get that?" my mom garbled through a mouthful of food. We all knew Bryce couldn't afford a cell phone on a pizza delivery boy's salary.

"Wage Warriors," Bryce murmured, not looking up from his plate.

"What's that?" I asked.

"It's…I joined…a guy at work. It's just a group," he said.

My mom's radar was rising. "You mean a gang?" she challenged.

Bryce sighed and closed his eyes. "It's just a group, no gang. We do things. I'm a part of something."

"What things?" I was challenging him now.

Bryce picked up the phone and started scrolling. "We make noise. You know, about the minimum wage."

"You mean protests?!" I nearly shot out of my chair with excitement. It still seemed so incongruous for my brother, the ultimate slacker and man of few words, to be a protester!

"So what do you need the phone for?" my mom asked.

"You know...meetings, flash mobs..."

"Flash mobs!" My mom's eyes were tinged with panic.

As if on cue, Bryce's phone vibrated. He stood up quickly and raised his finger. "I've got to take this," he said quickly, walking out of the room.

"Woo-hoo, Mr. Important!" I mocked.

My mom seemed to have aged in the past few minutes. I could see the firm line of her mouth as she vigorously scrubbed a crusty Pyrex dish at the sink.

Two weeks later, I awoke in the middle of the night to hear a grunting, scuffling and dragging sound in the hallway outside my room. I could hear my mom's voice and Bryce moaning lightly. I rose to get out of bed to look but something stopped me when I heard the door of Bryce's room squeak shut. I waited for a few minutes, my heart thudding and then willed myself into the hallway.

There was mom leaving Bryce's room with a bottle of rubbing alcohol and a bundle of bloody towels.

"What's going on?" I gasped.

"Luanne, get back to bed NOW!" mom rasped. "And don't go in there," she added with an admonishing but shaking finger at Bryce's door.

"As if I would anyway," I snapped. Bryce's room was off limits for as long as I could remember. I had rarely seen the door open, except during mom's periodic cleaning forays.

That entire weekend was a veil of secrecy. I overheard mom whispering on the kitchen phone to call in sick at the nursing home. The next two days she was constantly in and out of Bryce's room, practicing her nursing craft at home.

Late on Sunday night, I had fallen asleep on the family room couch when the cushion next to me jostled, knocking me awake. Looking down at my sprawled form was Bryce.

Or some alien version of him.

His right eye was swollen shut in the biggest shiner I've ever seen. He was breathing in slow rasps and grasping his ribs.

"Bryce! Are you all right? Mom wouldn't let me –"

"Shh!" He stopped me, a finger to his lips. He moaned lightly, leaning forward to turn on the X-Box.

"Bryce, what happened to you?" I was starting to become exasperated with his silence, although that was the norm for him.

Bryce winced and turned back to the X-Box. Just like the door to his room, the door to conversation was closed.

On getting ready for school that morning, I noticed Bryce was still on the couch but the X-Box had been replaced by CNN. I wanted to laugh, this brother who only watched Monster Truck shows and wrestling matches. No public affairs programming for this boy, no sir! He stiffly turned to look over his shoulder at me and then began to channel surf. I stood rooted to my spot behind him on the couch as a story of a flash mob mingled with a vicious police confrontation emerged in bursts and snips.

"It's your peeps, isn't it? Wage Warriors?" I clarified, as if that was even necessary.

Bryce never turned around.

Three weeks later, I came home from school to a deserted house – or so I thought. From the kitchen, I could hear a soft but intense conversation between Bryce and mom from Bryce's room.

"But it's dangerous! You know firsthand! It's not worth it, Bryce!"

"Mom, it's only for two days. I'll call you. I'm a part of something now!"

"Bryce, who's paying for all of this?"

"We get donations. We have…people. It's only Washington, not China! I told you, I'll be back in two days!"

"Well, I don't like this. What if you get arrested?"

Bryce laughed dryly. "What if? What if? I'm so tired of 'what if' and just being stuck!"

"Does Pizza Shack know?"

There was a pause. "No. But they will."

Ten minutes later, Bryce and mom came slowly out of his room. I started as I saw Bryce. My perpetually disheveled brother's hair was neatly combed (gasp! Was that styling gel as well?). He was dressed in a crisp, white open-collared shirt with dress pants and a dark windbreaker. He held a backpack.

"Luanne, your brother is going to Washington, D.C. with the Wage Warriors for a meeting to discuss raising the minimum wage." My mom's tone was oddly formal and her voice trembled.

"You mean a protest?" I countered.

Bryce smiled. His face looked thinner and his shiner was now a dull, yellow patch. The eye on that side was back open but narrower, giving him a more serious, contemplative look.

"Do you need a ride to the bus?" mom asked.

"I can walk," Bryce said.

"Don't go," my mom said abruptly.

"I'm a part of something now," said Bryce, swinging open the screen door and thudding down the porch steps.

A phone ringing at a certain hour always seems to have more impact or urgency.

"Yes, this is Laverne Franklin," my mom said quietly into the phone.

I walked quietly to her side.

"What?! Are you sure? Where? Are you sure it's him?!" As if in slow motion, I watched her sink into the faded beige vinyl chair that had attended the kitchen landline for as long as I could remember.

I drifted into the family room in front of the muted TV, promptly bringing up the volume to camouflage my mom's cries and pleas for information. My legs felt like gelatin as I dropped onto the couch, ever mindful of the permanent furrow created on the sofa cushion next to me by my slacker brother. I raised my eyes to the TV, hearing of Wage Warriors chained to White House fences but also noting some that were mobile, shouting and scuffling. The parade of channels revealed teargas from the Capitol Police and then gunshots. Without seeing him, I knew Bryce was both gone and at the epicenter of it all.

I rose after some time and walked stiffly (really hobbled) down the hallway toward my room. On the way, I noticed Bryce's bedroom door open an inch or two. It caught my attention because of the rarity of seeing that door even slightly ajar and because the light coming from it was the only light on a pre-dawn as black as Pittsburgh coal. I started shuffling again. The last thing I heard before closing my bedroom door was the strident voice of a southern Senator or other political-type coming from the vacated TV:

"But the minimum wage was NEVER MEANT to live on…"

THE VISIT

My fingers hurt as I placed a thumb tack through the top of the neatly lettered index card. I was placing it on a corkboard in the lobby of First Baptist Church as I left services that Sunday. The corkboard was a communication point for parishioners – youngsters requesting babysitting jobs, Vacation Bible School flyers, requests for rides needed here and there and the like. I looked at the index card I had tacked up as I absently kneaded the sore joints on my hand. I was finally requesting help at my home this summer. I was only sixty years old but my arthritis seemed to have worsened by a quantum leap this past year. I simply needed help, mostly outdoors. I briefly thought about the moment of panic I'd had a week earlier when I had trouble getting up for several minutes after working on my knees in the garden. Ten years earlier, I could spend the entire day from dawn to dusk in the garden with no physical effects beyond fatigue.

As I walked to my car, I felt a wave of loneliness. I had been widowed for nineteen years and lost my only child twenty years ago. It never got easier. The longing never went away.

I lived alone in a farmhouse on three acres with a small barn and a large vegetable garden. Flower gardens rimmed the entire perimeter of the house. I had also built up three berms blooming with various flowering bushes in my pre-arthritic freedom. After changing from my church clothes into jeans and a t-shirt, I took a seat on the shady wraparound porch with the newspaper. I was isolated here, both physically and socially. My only company were the birds most days.

I watched as a forest green Jeep Wrangler made it down the dusty B-highway in front of my house. I straightened in my chair as the Jeep came to a stop on the side of the road. A young man stepped out and started walking up my driveway. As he came closer, I revised my impression from young man to teenager. He stopped at the bottom of the porch steps and shaded his eyes with his hand to look up at me.

"Can I help you?" I called down to him.

"Yes, ma'am," he replied politely. "Are you Alma Pendleton?"

"Yes, I am."

"Ms. …Mrs. …" He seemed lost in how to properly address me.

"Mrs.," I offered.

"Mrs. Pendleton, I saw your card on the bulletin board at church."

I was surprised. "Oh, I just put that up this morning."

The young man was tall and rangy in a plaid shirt, jeans and a well-worn pair of cowboy boots. He put both hands in his back pockets and rocked subtly back and forth on his heels.

"You interested in the job?"

"Yes, ma'am."

"What's your name?"

"I'm Cole. Cole Watts."

I stood up and ambled down the porch steps to shake his hand. He took my hand very gently and shyly. His blue eyes and shock of unruly black hair vaguely reminded me of my late husband Jack but mixed in with someone else familiar that I couldn't quite identify in the moment.

"How old are you, Cole?"

"I'm seventeen."

"Oh, do your mom and dad know you're applying here?"

Cole's eyes shyly shifted from me to the ground. His hands went back into his back jean pockets. "Uh, no. And it's just my mama."

"Well, Cole, I'm going to tell you all about the job. If we make an arrangement, I will want to talk to your mama. Agreed?"

"Yes, ma'am, agreed."

We began to walk toward the barn and vegetable garden as I talked.

"Cole, my arthritis is starting to get the better of me. I'm going to need a lot of help this summer. As you can see, this is a big lot. I need someone to cut grass. There's a self-propelled mower in the barn. I warn you, it's not a riding mower, so you'll be sweating."

I gestured toward the garden. "This will also consume your days. I grow almost anything you can put in a salad or cook up. Weeding, watering, harvesting, monitoring for pests…you name it! I also pride myself on my flowers but I just can't tolerate tending to them on my hands and knees any longer." We were now on the side of the farmhouse, looking at the flowers planted there.

Cole nodded. He was very still as I spoke, indeed a careful listener.

"If we get a rainy day, you can work in the barn. The tools in there are in a mess and need to be organized. I can also use help around the house with vacuuming and dusting. Oh, and there's a room you could paint for me." I realized that my language had shifted into addressing Cole as an employee when he had actually hardly spoken yet. I paused and re-grouped. "Are you interested in the job, Cole?" I posed.

"Ma'am, I really need this job. I'm headed to college in Amherst in the fall. I'm a scholarship student but there's still books and all kinds of living expenses."

"Congratulations and good for you!" I replied. "Cole Watts, you've got the job!"

He smiled as if I'd just given him the moon.

"Now Cole, I expect you to be here every day from 8 AM until 4:30 PM, sharp, just as if you were punching a time clock. I pay $20 per hour. I don't tolerate being late. But if you're sick, don't come. As you can see, I'm getting older and my immune system isn't what it used to be."

Cole nodded, continuing to listen in his still, careful manner.

I went on. "Lunch is included every day. If you arrive early, I'll include breakfast. Oh, and I'll need your phone number to talk to your mama. Let's go back to the house so I can get a pen."

Cole wrote "Katie Watts" on a slip of paper and her phone number.

"Because you're still a minor, I'd like to talk to your mama. Is this a cell phone number?"

"Uh, no. My mama only has a landline."

"Oh, well, then. I'll try to catch her at home. When's a good time to reach her?"

Cole paused, thinking. "She's a nurse, so her shifts change week to week. This week she's on nights, so try her around mid-morning. She's usually still up around 10 AM or so. But I know she's off today."

"Okay. Thank you, Cole. When can you start?"

Cole smiled expansively and threw his hands up in the air. "How about now?"

It was almost 3 PM, but we agreed that Cole would work two hours. He would start with weeding and watering the garden and then begin to mow the grass.

I watched him work for a few minutes from the porch. He was a very calm but diligent and efficient worker. He was intent and linear in his tasks, not sidetracked as some in his age group were. He seemed very familiar in his looks, speech and movements, but I couldn't place him.

I went inside to call Cole's mother. This call would also serve as a sort of reference check, albeit from a biased source. I was fairly confident that Cole didn't have any dark surprises. "Now, watch," I dialogued within myself. "You'll call and his mama will tell you he's a car thief right out of juvie!" I shook my head at this ridiculous thought.

The line was busy. It occurred to me that I hadn't heard a busy signal in quite some time. How could Cole's mother function without a cell phone, I wondered. I was no tech junkie but I certainly wasn't a sixty year-old Luddite either.

I looked out the window. Cole was bringing the lawn mower out of the barn. It then dawned on me that Cole didn't appear to have a cell phone either. Most teenagers brandished them constantly, like an appendage. I wondered if Cole had a cell phone in the Jeep and just had the decency to leave it there as he worked. I decided that this was probably the correct answer as Cole seemed to be an uncommon teenager indeed.

Over the next two weeks, our arrangement went swimmingly. The grounds hadn't looked this good in many years. My only regret is that I hadn't asked for help sooner. Cole easily completed the work of three people in his quiet way. The only loose end was that I couldn't reach his mama. The line was perpetually busy. One afternoon during lunch on the porch, Cole stood up to remove a folded piece of paper from his jeans. "Oh, I almost forgot, Mrs. Pendleton. My mama wrote you a note. I told her you wanted to speak to her and couldn't reach her on the phone."

"Oh, thank you, Cole." I took the note and read it aloud. The script was schoolteacher perfect:

> Dear Mrs. Pendleton,
>
> Thank you for the work you are providing for my son Cole this summer. We both deeply appreciate it. I apologize for being difficult to reach but my shifts keep changing. I would like to meet you sometime. Please let me know if you have any questions or concerns. If you like, you can send a note home with Cole.
>
> Best,
> Kathleen Watts

I giggled internally, thinking of pinning a note to Cole's shirt to take home to mama, just like a kindergartner.

It rained torrentially for two solid days in mid-July. Cole was occupied painting a spare room that I planned to convert into a home office when I called him for lunch.

I was stirring soup on the stove when he walked into the family room. "Lunch in two minutes," I called to him over my shoulder. In that brief look, I saw Cole approaching the fireplace mantle. The mantle was virtually a shrine to my deceased family with photos of my late husband Jack and my late son Francis. Cole picked up a photo of Francis and stared at it quietly. This was the last photo I had of Francis, taken one month before he died. His dark hair was hanging comically into his brown eyes and his cheeks had the pink flush of healthy youth. It occurred to me that Cole and I had never spoken about my family, but I felt a flash of panic in not wanting to go there now.

I was serving the soup at the kitchen table when Cole shyly approached me with the picture of Francis in his hands.

"Mrs. Pendleton, who is this?"

I felt almost out of my body in that moment. To my own disbelief, I wordlessly snatched the photo from his hands and replaced it on the mantle. When I arrived back in the kitchen, Cole looked stunned and wounded.

"Ma'am, I'm sorry I-" he began.

"Sit down and eat," I commanded him, more harshly than I intended.

We slurped our soup in silence.

I softened, feeling immediately and deeply sorry for my flash of temper. I diverted. "Oh, look, it's finally clearing up. You may be able to do some weeding in the garden after all today. Just don't track mud into the house."

Cole silently stood up and left the table, exiting onto the porch.

I sighed and rubbed my eyes. I then got up and joined him at the porch railing. He was staring out at the road in front of the house. Steam was rising from the slick asphalt.

This time I had a photo in my hands. It was our final photo together as a family, taken twenty two years ago.

"Okay, Cole, I'm sorry, but you blindsided me in there."

"I'm so sorry, ma'am."

"Don't be." I held up the photo. "You might recognize me. This is my son Francis." I jabbed a finger at the road. "He died twenty years ago right in front of this house. He was playing catch with me and the ball went out into the street. Before I could warn him, he was hit by a semi-truck." I closed my eyes, thinking of Francis on the asphalt with an obvious skull fracture. I remembered his white t-shirt starting to look like a hideous tie-die as the blood seeped out of him. I went on. "And this is Jack, my late husband. A year after Francis died, I found him dead in bed. The doctor said it was a massive heart attack. I say it was a broken heart. So now you know."

Cole continued to look at the road in silence as if picturing the whole scenario. "I am so deeply sorry, Mrs. Pendleton," he said, just above a whisper. "I'm sure you were a great wife and mother. They were lucky to have you."

As I looked at Cole through a veil of tears, I knew that Kathleen Watts was the lucky one.

August always seemed to come quickly but never more so than this year. They say that time passing ever more quickly is a sign of aging. I knew it was something else.

"Well, one more time," I said to Cole. We were lounging on the porch having lemonade before he left for the day. Cole's last shift for the summer was tomorrow.

"When do you leave for college?"

"Saturday."

"Oh. Day after tomorrow."

"Yup."

"So what's next for you at Amherst, Cole?"

"Well, I'm going to study liberal arts. Then I'm thinking about going to divinity school."

"Oh, you mean become a minister or a pastor?"

"Yeah, something like that."

I nodded. It all made sense. The kind, quiet, careful listener would make a superb clergyman.

"Cole, you can come back at winter break. I'll have jobs for you inside the house and you can shovel snow for me."

Cole nodded and listened in his still, careful manner.

"And I hope you'll come back for the summer next year. Same job. Maybe a few more dollars an hour. You're worth it. Really."

Cole stood up, hands in his back pockets. "You've been more than generous to me, Mrs. Pendleton."

"Aw, call me Alma."

Cole smiled and walked down the porch steps. "See you tomorrow morning," he called over his shoulder.

I waved. One more time, I thought.

But it wasn't to be. Cole called at 7 AM saying he would not be reporting for work, something about car trouble.

"But I'm sending someone in my place to help you."

I gasped, once again realizing that Cole's care and concern seemed without limits.

"Don't worry," he continued. "Most of my major work is done, so you should be in good shape. This will be someone you know and love!"

I was intrigued. Who could this be? I had lived quite an isolated life over the past two decades.

Cole went on. "He'll arrive at 12:00 noon and leave promptly at 4:30 PM, not a second later. He'll actually disappear at 4:30, okay? So don't worry about him or look for him. He just has to leave right on time."

I didn't quite follow what Cole was saying but I went along. We wrapped up our phone call with promises to stay in touch during the semester. I reviewed my proposal of his continued employment over winter and summer breaks from school. Then we said our goodbyes.

After Cole hung up the phone, he held the small timer in his hands. He knew the rules: one person, one visit only (no future or repeat visits), up to a four and one half hour time frame in duration. Four and one half hours was pushing it, Cole realized as he set the timer, but any shorter duration might seem cruel or too perfunctory. 4:30 was a good departure time. Cole always felt sad when people disappeared after dark.

At 11:58 AM, I sat on the porch awaiting my substitute helper. I didn't have a name, but any friend of Cole's was likely to be a stellar worker. I looked out at the road patiently. I noticed a little boy walking down the middle of the road. He seemed to be looking here and there for something. I wanted to tell him to walk on the side of the road for his own safety. God knows that people always drove too fast on this road and came out of nowhere.

But then I saw who it was.

Francis?!

By then, he was running toward me. He was clad in the very clothes he had died in twenty years ago, except the t-shirt was again pristine white.

"Mama!" he called out to me.

I ran on shaky legs out onto the lawn where five year-old Francis stood. I hoped I wouldn't faint as I knelt on the grass to listen to him. I hugged him, smelling the dryer sheets I used twenty years ago on his t-shirt. Francis was undeniably alive with clear eyes and flushed cheeks. I could feel his heart beating a mile a minute as I embraced him.

"Mama, I can't find the ball!" His little brow was furrowed in frustration.

Then I saw the ball. It was torn and completely flattened in the middle of the street as if run over by a …

I froze. Dear God, I thought. He's picking up right where we left off! He doesn't know what really happened!

I placed my hands gently on Francis' cheeks. "Honey, listen. New rules. I'll get a different ball but we have to play only in the backyard. That way we don't lose the ball anymore!" (Or your life, I thought). I was amazed at how quickly I snapped back into parenting and motherly problem-solving after a two decade hiatus.

The afternoon passed in several rounds of catch in the backyard. I even found Francis' old inflatable wading pool in the barn and we dangled our legs while enjoying popsicles and ice cream.

Before I knew it, the time was 3 PM. Only ninety minutes left. It all seemed impossible.

"Come on, Francis. Time to help mama with supper!"

Francis frowned. "It's too early for supper, mama," he retorted.

"Well, then how about we call it lunch?" I took his plump little hand and we bounded back into the house. I couldn't bear sending him away without having supper.

After a childhood feast of macaroni and cheese with hot dogs and more ice cream, I snuck a look at the kitchen clock as Francis prattled on about a frog he saw earlier today. He was wondering aloud how the frog would like the little wading pool.

The time was 4:27 PM. Three minutes left. I had to think quickly. Then it came to me.

"How about another game?" I said, leading Francis back out onto the porch.

"What game?"

"Hide and seek!"

"Oh, I'm good at that game!"

"I know you are, honey!" I looked at my watch, trying not to cry. 4:29 PM. "How about a hug? Then I'll count to twenty with my eyes closed while you hide."

The hug was cruelly quick because Francis was eagerly awaiting my countdown.

As I counted, I kept two fingers slightly apart over my eyes. I saw Francis giggle, looking this way and that. Then he disappeared around the side of the house.

I stopped counting and stayed on the porch steps for another hour. It was perfectly quiet except for a light breeze and the crickets.

I phoned Cole in Amherst to see how mid-term exams went. He seemed pleased with his performance, but the logic class was harder than expected. We exchanged pleasantries and I encouraged him to stay in touch as his time permitted.

Neither of us mentioned the visit. It was understood.

Cole didn't come home for winter break, citing financial trouble with travel expenses. I was disappointed but I understood. As it turned out, I didn't need a snow shoveler because the winter was inexplicably mild.

The last time I spoke to Cole was in late April. He was so sorry, but he wasn't coming home from Amherst this summer at all because he had one course to take and a job waiting for him at the yacht club.

"They're lucky to have you!" These were among my last words to Cole.

That spring, I placed another index card on the corkboard at church. As I left, I knew one thing.

Lightning doesn't strike twice.

INSPIRATION

I retired from my job as an investment banker after thirty five years right into a second career as a free-lance writer. Two years into "retirement," I had published two novels that were selling well regionally. My husband Walt and I lived on the east side of Milwaukee. We also had a vacation retreat in the form of a two bedroom faux log cabin in Gill's Rock in the peaceful reaches of northernmost Door County. Walt was still working as an attorney in the Third Ward so our Gill's Rock residence was mostly limited to weekend use. However, I periodically went there alone, primarily to write in the silence. This was one of those times. I had arrived at the cabin on Tuesday to write. Walt was driving up on Friday afternoon along with Marnie and David, two friends of ours from Chicago, to spend the weekend. Life was good.

But the writing part lately was not. Since my arrival Tuesday noon, I had not been able to write a single word. This was highly unusual for me as I could sometimes produce twenty to thirty pages per day if not unduly interrupted.

I had read a bit about "writer's block" in my writing magazines but I never gave it much thought. I knew it to be a very real phenomenon, though. I remembered a woman from my on-line writer's group who sustained an eighteen month dry spell. We tried to encourage her on our weekly Zoom calls but to no avail. She finally quit the group. I'll never forget her remarks during our last meeting: "Maybe I don't have anything more to say in writing. Some authors only have one book in them." While historically true and accurate, I remember pitying the woman's comment but secretly cheering that it wasn't me.

Now here I sat in the warmth and comfort of the cabin in Gill's Rock. It was now Friday noon and I had not been able to write a single syllable. It was the literary equivalent of lockjaw. I was looking forward to seeing Walt, Marnie and David for welcome relief from this empty, restless week. Part of me was scared. This could very well be the end of my writing. What would I do then? Go back to investment banking? Take up knitting? Get a dog or two? Walt was certainly not retiring any time soon.

My cell phone ringing jolted me out of my reverie. It was Walt. "Hey, I just hit the road," he said, talking much too loud as he always did in the car. "I should be there before dark. I don't plan to stop if I can help it, but there's a huge snowstorm coming."

"Just be careful, Walt."

"So how are you?"

"Uh, okay. Defrosting chicken for tonight. Still not writing."

There was a pause on Walt's end. Then he said, "Rita, maybe you're pushing yourself too hard. Maybe you just need a rest."

"Yeah, maybe."

"Okay, I'll see you between 4:30 and 5:00."

"Be careful, Walt."

We parted.

Our guest bedroom was also a library and writing room for me. I wandered in and began randomly selecting books from the shelves and tossing them on the glossy oak desk. Great Expectations. Leaves of Grass. The Aeneid. The Godfather. The Bible. The Fountainhead.

I sat down at the desk, books piled on either side of me. I knew that reading sometimes inspired writing. I cracked open "The Fountainhead" and wondered what the literary giants did when or if they encountered writer's block. What did Ayn Rand or Walt

Whitman do in the face of a dearth of ideas? Did they ever have a dearth of ideas?

I woke up two hours later, my head down on the desk, books still piled up silently around me. I looked out the window. The light had changed. It was now 2:00 in the afternoon.

I yawned and stretched, deciding that fresh air would be the next best tactic for me. I walked to a local shop to purchase a pound of smoked whitefish. By the time I started walking back to the cabin, it had started to snow rather thickly.

I had ventured out in a fleece vest versus a true winter coat, so I immediately brushed the copious snowflakes from me before entering the cabin. Then I sat at the kitchen table and began noshing on smoked fish and Ritz crackers – a guilty pleasure of mine.

I reached over and turned on the stereo for an FM radio station. Terrestrial radio in greater Milwaukee was virtually devoid of classical music, but not so in Door County. Debussy's piano filtered into my kitchen with the quiet, poignant notes of Clair de Lune. Someone once wrote on the Internet that this composition would be playing at the end of the universe as the credits rolled. I put my head in my hands. This piece could inspire a monkey to write! But not me…

At 3:10 PM, I received a call from Walt from the road.

"Wow, Rita, it's really getting slick out here. The visibility is terrible!" he said, still too loudly.

"Be careful, Walt. Maybe you need to turn around?" (I really didn't want him to take me up on that offer as I wanted him here).

"No, it's okay. I'll just take my time. I'll stop if I need to. Oh, and Rita?"

"Yes?"

"Marnie and David called. They won't be coming this weekend due to the weather."

I was mildly disappointed but time alone with Walt was always welcome.

Walt came in the door at 5:40 PM, dropping his duffel immediately to enfold me in a hug. Then he fished in one of the upper kitchen cupboards to retrieve a sauce pan. He set it on the stove. I knew at once what that meant – Walt's homemade cocoa, a literal festival of chocolate that tasted like hot liquid fudge. And he made it properly – on the stovetop with actual chunks of chocolate and whole milk, not a gummy instant packet in the microwave.

"It's cold in here. How do you stand it?" Walt blew on his fingertips as I sliced chicken. "I'll go get some firewood from the shed."

The fieldstone fireplace was yet another handsome feature of our faux log cabin – functional, too.

However, after several seconds, Walt stuck just his head inside the front door with an impish expression on his eternally boyish face, no firewood in sight. "It's good packing snow…" he opened.

That was our code for a snowball fight! I abandoned my raw chicken and ran out into this spectacular snow globe of a Door County night.

Walt already had a well-formed softball-sized snowball in his hand. In the starlight, I saw it arc toward me. It then smacked me in the forehead, not hurting me but catching me off balance. The next thing I knew I was stumbling backward into the snow.

"Rita! I'm sorry! Bad aim! Are you okay?" Walt hovered above me.

I laughed. "I'm just fine!" I breathed in the cold air and my sixty five year-old self began making a snow angel, taking definite advantage of my fall.

Walt had always been a kid at heart. He dropped down beside me, making his own snow angel after inadvertently kicking me with his foot twice.

I stopped and looked up at the eternal stars.

Then it happened.

Ideas.

They began to inundate me in quick fashion, like quasars or shooting stars.

It wasn't all over after all.

It was just beginning.

THE SATURDAY VISITOR

It's not every day that you get a letter from God. Call me delusional, but that's exactly what happened to me. I was in my late 20s living in an apartment outside of Chicago. The week before I received the letter, I'd had a nasty break-up with my on-again, off-again boyfriend of three years, Derrick.

The letter was inconspicuously mingled in among a flyer for a lawn service and my cable bill. The cursive looked antiquated on the envelope, as if written with a feather pen. There was no return address but a small emblem of a star on the back of the envelope. Inside was a thick cream-colored piece of paper stating the following:

Dear Blair,

You have been specially selected to receive a weekly four-hour visit from a beloved but departed family member of my choosing. I only make this offer once every one thousand years and to only one person on each of the seven earthly continents. My offer comes with the following conditions:

(1) I will choose the family member based upon your current life circumstances.

(2) Visits will occur every Saturday between 12:00 noon to 4:00 PM.

(3) If you need to cancel a visit, simply include it in your prayers.

(4) Visits will occur for the remainder of your natural life (i.e. indefinitely) unless you request them to cease.

(5) This may be the most important condition of all: No one can see or interact with your visitor EXCEPT FOR YOU. This includes phone conversations, social media, texts, letters, photographs, glimpses through a window or any other intentional or unintentional form of communication. If anyone else interacts with or sees your visitor, all future visits will be canceled.

(6) Your visitor will automatically appear in your home at 12:00 noon and disappear from your home at 4:00 PM. I recommend closing all blinds and pulling all window shades for all visits to maintain a private, confidential atmosphere.

(7) If you are out of town or on vacation, your visitor will continue to arrive every Saturday at the same time. However, out of town or vacation visits are strongly discouraged given the increased risk of discovery in an unfamiliar or less familiar environment. Please use the discretion you have received from me in order to make the safest decision. Also, no need to notify me of your leaving town. (After all, I am God).

(8) No property or material gifts may be exchanged between you and your visitor. The true gift is each other's renewed company. Food and beverage may be consumed as desired while together.

I realize that my conditions are many and may make this seem like a sterile or daunting process, but I assure you that you will find it to be the most rewarding experience of your life should you proceed. Please take all of the time you need to make a decision. I have eternity. If you have any questions or wish to convey your decision, simply pray them up to me.

Love,
God

P.S. Blair, have compassion for Derrick. He is a very troubled young man. I had to remove him for your own safety and well-being.

Again,
Love,
God

I sank onto the couch, flabbergasted for lack of a better word. If this was a hoax, it was a most elaborate one. What did I have to lose? My job as a speech-language pathologist in an outpatient clinic involved periodic weekends, so I was home on most Saturdays. (In fact, I was home quite a lot since breaking up with Derrick, licking my wounds).

So I prayed up. It went like this: "What do I have to lose, God? Send him/her. You have lots of choices since my entire immediate family is deceased – mom, dad, brother, sister, grandma, grandpa. Also, when?"

Nothing happened at first. Twenty minutes later, I was unloading the dishwasher when the word "tomorrow" popped into my mind.

Tomorrow was Saturday.

My nerves were quaking on Saturday as I readied the apartment for my visitor. Who did God have in store? Who could it be? My dad, younger sister Myra and younger brother James were killed eight years ago on the expressway by a drunk driver on their way home from a Cubs game. My mother followed them three years ago, right around the time I started dating Derrick. Breast cancer sealed her fate. Grandma and Grandpa both died peacefully in old age.

If it was my dad, I had an enormous plate of cheese and crackers – his hands-down favorite – awaiting in the kitchen. If it was mom, I was prepared to discuss in detail the last three books I read. If it was Myra, I had my phone set up so we could dance like we were clubbing. Should it be James, I looked up the time and channel for the Cubs broadcast. If Grandma or Grandpa showed up, the photo albums awaited to tweak their affections for nostalgia.

It was 11:58 AM. I went into the bathroom to check my hair and clothes. I sighed nervously into the mirror. "It's only family, don't worry," I whispered to my startled reflection. I closed my eyes briefly and then resolutely exited the bathroom.

Then I saw him. His back was to me, bent over the plate of cheese and crackers in the kitchen.

My dad.

He turned around and smiled with his lips closed, cheeks already bulging with cheese and crackers. He held up a cracker. "What kind of crackers are these?" he garbled through his mouthful. "Mmm. So buttery!"

Then I was hugging him as my tears flowed involuntarily.

"Don't cry, Blair," my dad soothed, his warm hands clasping my shoulders. "It's been eight years! Look at you! You are so beautiful!

And this is a happy day. We'll have every Saturday together from now on!"

I regarded my dad. He looked much like he did when I last saw him, his wavy brown hair combed back and his soft brown eyes crinkled into a smile. He wore a casual suit with a turtleneck. My dad was always smartly dressed, the only exception being when he cut grass or worked on cars. Then he would change into a faded blue sweatshirt with the sleeves roughly hacked off.

It was surreal as my dad and I sat down on the couch together in the living room. I turned on the light so I could see him better. Despite the noonday sun, the apartment was quite dark given the necessity to draw all of the blinds and curtains. How do you catch up on eight long years apart? We were about to find out.

As the afternoon progressed, the conversation drew like a magnet to the topic of Derrick.

"I probably don't need to tell you much about him or us because you already know. Right, dad?" I asked as I sliced more cheese into petite squares.

"I don't see everything you're doing – frame by frame, minute to minute," my dad replied. "It's more broad strokes. I get more the gist of what's going on, big picture stuff. So, shoot!"

I tearfully relayed the mess of my past three years with Derrick. It started off well. I met Derrick shortly before my mom died. He was actually a physical therapy patient at our clinic. He would saunter over to the speech therapy office, right off the main gym, and make conversation with me if I wasn't with a patient. He was recovering from an athletic injury that resulted in knee surgery. Then my mom died and I was out of the clinic for a while. I never thought I'd see Derrick again because his course of care was almost over. But he found me on Facebook and showed up in the lobby of my apartment building one day. His hair was always neatly combed, his shirt tucked in just so. He usually wore a tie in the early days when he came to see me. I used to joke with him that he looked like a door-to-door salesman.

Derrick was completely there for me after mom passed. We didn't begin with dates so much as running errands together. He was a wonderful cook and made sure I ate plentifully in my grief. Then he moved in with me the fall after mom died.

Our lives continued in harmony until Derrick started calling in sick to work. His boss at the oil change place was a very accommodating guy, but you can only call in with the flu so many times before suspicion takes over. Derrick was then fired and began to languish around the apartment as I went out into the world each day.

In the early going, he would always have a sumptuous meal ready for me when I arrived home from the clinic. He looked freshly showered and even wore a tie sometimes at dinner. When I asked if he looked for work that day, he would summarily reply with a cheerful "no."

Several months into Derrick's unemployment, I noticed that the apartment was starting to look dirty and shabby. My feet would stick to the kitchen floor in spots. Scratch cooking for dinner turned into pizza in the fridge that had already been partially eaten. Derrick was unshaven most days and his neatly combed hair gave way to stringy dishevelment.

One evening after another half-hearted dinner of cold pizza, I asked him what was wrong. He just shrugged. I pressed, sitting closer to him on the couch. It was then that I smelled it. Weed. Undeniably. When I looked into his eyes, I saw a crisscross of bloody vessels and deeply dilated pupils.

"Are you stoned?!" I said, incredulous.

"It's no big deal. Just a couple blunts. C'mon, do you think I like what's going on lately?"

That led to our first of many knock-down, drag-out, epic arguments. Derrick sequestered himself in the bathroom as I pounded on the door, refusing to give up on expressing my point that it was entirely expected and within his power to not only look for but hold a job!

The bathroom door in my apartment does not have a lock but it sticks shut sometimes. When Derrick didn't reply, I felt I had no choice and I shouldered my way in.

Derrick was sitting on the toilet tank looking startled. In his hands was a bottle of something called Oxycodone. It was at least half empty. Later that evening, I found five more empty bottles of Oxycodone in his gym bag, all from different physicians and pharmacies. Derrick was indeed shopping and addicted.

I made an ultimatum that night. I kicked him out, stating that he was not welcome in my life until he had completed rehabilitation and secured a job. Derrick started to cry, pleading with me not to shut him out. He stated that the Oxycodone temporarily got out of hand after his knee surgery but that he was simply not a "stoner" or a drug addict. Then he left for the first time.

I took Derrick back the following year. He had checked all of the boxes. Rehab? Done. He even belonged to a Narcotics Anonymous support group and had a sponsor there named Nathan. You better believe I phoned Nathan for verification! Job? Yup! Derrick was working at Kwik Trip as a cashier. He looked good – impeccably groomed and rested but his neck ties seemed to have gone into the past. Oh, well. I was pleased to have him move back in and become part of my life again.

The first year after that was great. We picked up largely where we left off on the good components of our relationship. Derrick went to work and to meetings. He resumed cooking with gourmet gusto for me. Then, one morning, he called in sick, stating that his back hurt. I remembered Derrick telling me the day before that he had lifted dozens of bags of ice melt salt at Kwik Trip and had "tweaked" his back. I told him to feel better and I went to work at the therapy clinic.

Business was slow that day at the clinic. My supervisor could usually provide additional patients on short notice because our clinic was attached to an inpatient hospital. However, the patient census was low there also. I was sent home at 2:30 instead of 5:30.

As I turned my key in the door, I could hear music thumping

inside. I made a mental note to remind Derrick to keep it down. I remembered hoping Derrick's back was better as I entered.

I called his name and walked into the living room. I could see Derrick's head from the back of the couch. There was another head next to his, though. The stench of weed was rampant. I whirled around to the front of the couch to behold a stoned, slouching Derrick sitting beside an equally stoned, slouching young man.

"Oh, hi, Blair. You're home early," Derrick slurred.

The other guy started to laugh, a giggle with little snorts, actually.

Derrick playfully and clumsily smacked his companion on the chest. "Hey, Blair, did you ever meet Nathan? He's my brother from another mother!"

Both of them dissolved into more snorting giggles as I stormed out of the room. I went into our bedroom and pulled down a suitcase from our closet shelf. It wasn't my suitcase. I was saving Derrick some trouble by packing for him.

I am ashamed to say that I actually took Derrick back two more times before finally cutting off our relationship last week. The last straw: Was it finding strangers stoned and messing up the kitchen after a hard day at work? No, actually not. Was it Derrick losing three more jobs? Believe it or not, no. You know what really ended it? It was finding a solitary syringe behind the toilet tank as I mopped the bathroom floor one Saturday. Derrick had graduated.

On to the university of heroin.

My dad sighed at the end of this emotionally blistering account.

"Dad, did I do the right thing? Should I have tried to help him more?"

My dad steepled his fingers in thought. "It seems that Derrick doesn't know what he wants, beyond drugs, of course. When you don't know what you want, you can't be in a relationship."

My dad's clarity astounded me.

"I mean, I kicked him out and took him back so many times. Am I stupid or what?"

My dad smiled with a tinge of sadness. "No, no, no. You are proud and smart. You made the best decisions for both of you."

I wiped another free-falling tear. "Dad, I'm so glad we get to do this!"

"Me, too, sweetheart. And this is just the beginning."

I glanced at the clock. 3:55. My dad would be going soon. I was so congested from crying that I excused myself to the bathroom to retrieve a tissue. When I came back out, my dad was gone.

As I picked up the now empty cheese and crackers platter, I felt momentarily guilty for dominating the conversation this afternoon. I also considered what a rare gift from God I was receiving – one that only six others were receiving in their respective time zones throughout the earth.

Needless to say, Saturday quickly became the pinnacle of the week for me. I would make ready ever-increasing platters of cheese and crackers. My dad would promptly arrive at noon and we would get right to our agenda. My dad was a huge cinema buff, so we spent many Saturdays looking at movies, ranging from old classics such as "Splendor In The Grass" (Look how young Natalie Wood and Warren Beatty are!) to campy 1970s disaster epics such as "The Poseidon Adventure" and "The Towering Inferno" with their star-studded but badly acting casts. My dad's other snack passion was popcorn and we would go through bowl after bowl as the movies rolled. I remembered attending movies at our hometown theatre with my dad as a child. In winter, he would wear a bulky parka and smuggle a large Hefty bag full of popcorn underneath it into the theatre. (He called the theatre popcorn prices "highway robbery"). When the lights went down, he would tap me on the shoulder and subtly unzip his parka to reveal a three-hour supply of popcorn. There was so much butter on it that it would drip down onto our wrists! I remember my mom telling my dad to throw that "greasy old parka" into the wash after one of our movie outings.

My dad and I were reminiscing about how I had been traumatized by "The Poseidon Adventure" as a child. (Actually, I was both traumatized and fascinated by the premise of being trapped in a luxury liner capsized upside down by a rogue tidal wave. To this day, my brain has to make constant adjustments to interpret the characters' surroundings with everything upside down). We then heard a knock at the door. My dad looked at me, his cheeks stuffed with popcorn, and shrugged.

"We'll just ignore it," I whispered.

But the pounding became louder and more insistent. Whoever it was would not go away.

I put a finger to my lips and admonished my dad to be quiet and stay put. I approached the door and saw my neighbor Carolyn through the peephole. "Hey, Blair, just checking on you! I hear a man in there. Are you all right?"

Carolyn was my neighbor across the hall. We were about the same age. She had been a tremendous help, support and comic relief from the whole tense Derrick saga. She had been divorced for several years and was admittedly lonely. Her most frequent visitor was her mother Gloria, a pleasant, mellow woman in her mid-sixties. Gloria would often stay with Carolyn on the weekends. Sometimes they included me in their hilarious game nights and chick flick marathons. With these thin walls and doors, I could sometimes hear them giggling and hooting into the night. But I didn't mind. Any mirth in my life was completely welcome at the moment.

I opened the door just a crack to appease Carolyn. "I'm fine, Carolyn. Now isn't such a good time, though. Can we talk tonight?"

I knew I had made a potentially disastrous mistake when Carolyn apparently took this as an invitation to come on in. Her eyes went immediately to the kitchen table where my dad's suit was hanging on the chair. Her hand clamped to her mouth. "I knew it! You've got a man in here! Hey, it's not you-know-who, is it?"

I calculated that if Carolyn clocked her head a few degrees to the right, she would see my dad munching popcorn on the couch and then God would revoke our visitation privileges. Miraculously, she was so giddy about me having a "date" that her eyes stayed focused on my dad's suit.

"No, it's not Derrick," I hissed. "And it's not what you think. Can you please leave, though?" I was now pleading with her.

Carolyn elbowed me in the hip gamely on her way out. "Cramping your style, am I, sister?" She winked at me and sauntered back into the hall after extracting a promise from me to do a "tell-all" later. I closed the door quickly and slumped against it, a sigh escaping me.

"Close one," my dad observed.

"Whew! You're not kidding!"

"Well, come on back. You're missing Shelly Winters swimming in her evening gown!"

I quickly rejoined my dad on the couch.

Several Saturdays later, my dad and I pulled out the family photo albums. As the sole surviving immediate family member, I now possessed all of them. I wanted to improve my skills as family historian, so my dad was helping me identify people and locations in photos. He also made suggestions on arranging some of them chronologically as many of the older photos did not display dates.

Then the knocking on the door came. It was a furious, relentless pounding that startled both of us. I could hear Carolyn on the other side. She sounded distressed and unintelligible.

"Stay here," I firmly cautioned my dad, a photo album still sitting on his lap. He shrugged and loaded up another cracker with smoked Gouda.

I opened the door and immediately closed it behind me, stepping out into the hallway. Carolyn was indeed distressed and crying. She was actually pulling on her hair.

"Blair, my mom fainted in the kitchen! She's not breathing!"

Our clinic required CPR certification every two years as a condition of employment, so I swiftly went into emergency mode.

"Did you call 911?"

"Yeah, but what's taking so long?" Carolyn sobbed.

We entered Carolyn's apartment. Gloria was on the floor in the small galley kitchen, motionless and ashen in complexion. "I have to start CPR! Get the defibrillator!" I barked out sharply at Carolyn.

Carolyn gave me a clueless look as she sobbed.

"It's next to the fire extinguisher on the wall in the lobby downstairs. Now go!" I commanded.

Gloria was indeed pulseless and non-breathing. I began chest compressions, counting aloud to stay calm and focused.

Suddenly, a second voice began counting in sync with me. I whirled around. My dad was standing in back of me.

"Dad, you've got to go! They can't see you or –"

He silently held up a hand. "Blair, it's better if there's two of us." He positioned himself at Gloria's head to start rescue breathing.

So many conflicting emotions were short-circuiting through me at that moment that I prayed I would not go into cardiac arrest. By then, Carolyn had arrived with the defibrillator. I saw her confused expression as she took in my dad, wondering how he fit into the picture.

After several minutes of CPR and two shocks, Gloria was breathing again and had a strong pulse, although she was still unconscious. The paramedics arrived for transfer to the hospital. My dad, Carolyn and I followed the gurney to the back of the ambulance. Ever the gentleman, my dad helped Carolyn step up into the ambulance to ride with her mother. Then I turned to one of the remaining paramedics and a police officer to provide a brief summary of what had transpired.

When I turned around, my dad was gone. God was true to His word.

CONVERGENCE

The elevator doors couldn't open fast enough for Dr. Alan Graveer. As a cardiac surgeon, he was always in demand and therefore always in a hurry. He had just received a call from a colleague requesting a pre-surgical consult. Dr. Bloch had been apologetic on the phone. "Al, I know it's getting late, but I've got this 46 year-old patient at Mercy. He desperately needs a CABG. Came in Tuesday with his second MI. With my schedule, I couldn't fit him in for surgery for another week. I heard you had open time that jibes with the OR schedule tomorrow and..."

Dr. Graveer was never one for lengthy explanations. He had the gist. He agreed to operate on Dr. Bloch's patient tomorrow. All the pre-surgical testing was in order. He would do a quick pre-surgical consult and introduce himself to the patient tonight. Dr. Bloch practically gushed with gratitude. "Don't even think of paying for any golf on my watch next season!" he quipped. But Dr. Graveer didn't really care about golf. He preferred to pump iron alone at the gym versus probing hospital politics on the golf course.

Dr. Graveer had immediately left his office after speaking to Dr. Bloch. All he had was a room number (C416) and not the patient's name. After an interminable lag, the elevator doors finally opened onto Mercy Hospital's cardiac floor.

Dr. Graveer practically sprang from the elevator and walked briskly down the main corridor. His nurse practitioner Glenda often joked that she took four steps for every single step Dr. Graveer took. He carried a tablet under his arm. He was 6'3" with broad shoulders and a narrow, fit waist. His muscular arms rippled out of his short-sleeved scrub top, the product of daily one hour weightlifting and sometimes boxing sessions.

Dr. Graveer took a seat in the charting area and logged onto his tablet. He would first perform a chart review on patient C416 and then a brief pre-surgical consult. Dr. Graveer preferred all patient contact to be as brief as possible. Emotional attachments or friendships bred medical mistakes and errors in judgment in his opinion. He interacted with patients in the same brisk manner in which he walked. Also, Dr. Graveer thought of patients strictly as cases, not as multi-dimensional people. To him, a patient equaled whatever cardiac procedure was being performed – nothing more, nothing less. If a patient needed any kind of hand-holding, he passed them off to Glenda or to the floor RN.

"Oh, Dr. Graveer. Are you here to see C416?" A female voice sounded in back of him.

Dr. Graveer looked over his shoulder to behold Dot, a seasoned RN who was also more pragmatic than personal. She was retiring next year after thirty eight years in the trenches.

"Yes, I'm taking over for Dr. Bloch to get the ball rolling sooner," Dr. Graveer offered. "How's the patient?"

"Weak as a kitten but stable. I heard Dr. Bloch is really backed up."

"Yes, he felt it would be detrimental for the patient to wait for his schedule to open up."

"I agree. Also, family was making noise about transferring him to another hospital and not one in our system."

Dr. Graveer raised an eyebrow. Oh, the publicity nightmare that could be! He sighed as he scrolled down the patient roster to find C416. As he did this, he thought about the evening ahead. From here, he would hit the gym for an hour of lifting. Then home for his wife's fabulous lamb stew. Then early to bed because the surgery would be at 6 AM.

Dr. Graveer clicked on room number C416 on the patient roster to enter the patient's chart. His name was Hobart Polzinski.

Dr. Graveer froze. He was rarely still unless something threw him. And this did. Could this be him? He read further. His age was about right. Indeed, he still resided in Mauston where Dr. Graveer grew up. Hobart had been working as a diesel mechanic until his first heart attack occurred two years ago. There had been no surgical intervention at that time, just a plainspoken conversation with Dr. Bloch about losing weight (a lot, apparently, as Hobart had been morbidly obese), smoking cessation and better medication compliance, particularly those related to his diabetes. Hobart was a high school graduate, divorced, no kids. It was probably him.

Dr. Graveer stood up and tucked his tablet under his muscled arm. Patient = case and procedure. No more. Certainly no less. Quick visit, just the essentials, and then on to the gym, lamb stew and bed.

Dr. Graveer knocked and slid open the pocket door to Hobart's room.

"Mr. Polzinski? I'm Dr. Alan Graveer, cardiac surgery. I'll be performing your procedure tomorrow."

The man in the bed looked up at Dr. Graveer. It was indeed THE Hobart Polzinski, but the man in this bed looked beaten down by chronic illness. The only thing he had apparently beaten at all was the morbid obesity. This man looked small, sallow and shrunken in bed with frail, spindly arms and legs. He appeared far beyond his 46 chronological years. Dr. Graveer could hear the hiss of the oxygen flow in Hobart's nasal cannula.

"We'll be performing something called a CABG. That's shorthand for coronary artery bypass grafting." Dr. Graveer felt himself switch over to auto-pilot as he described the procedure, its risks and the immediate post-operative recovery period. "In a few days, you'll see my nurse practitioner, Glenda. She will get you referred to cardiac rehab. Okay, surgery is at 6 AM tomorrow. Nothing to eat or drink after midnight. I suggest you get some rest. Any questions?"

Hobart wearily maintained eye contact with Dr. Graveer. "I thought Dr. Bloch was going to do my surgery."

"Dr. Bloch called me. His schedule can't accommodate you until next week. He felt that the delay could be detrimental to you. If there's nothing else, I'll-"

Suddenly, Hobart smiled to reveal those crooked, overlapping, yellowed teeth. It was the same cruel smile that Hobart gave Alan Graveer in high school before some nasty put-down or before the first blow. Hobart seemed to be gathering strength. With a slight groan, he sat up on the edge of the bed to face Dr. Graveer.

"I wouldn't sit up right now, Mr. Polzinski. You need to rest. And don't try to get up by yourself. Use the call button to get help. You're a fall risk," Dr. Graveer prattled on, backing up slightly from Hobart.

"You go to Mauston High?"

"Yes. Now listen to me, you need to get all the way back into bed, Mr. Polzinski!"

Then he laughed. That same nasty cackle that preceded and/or followed a beating or bullying back in high school. "'Mr. Polzinski'?" Hobart mocked. "Al, this is me, Hobie!"

"I know who you are."

Hobart pointed to Dr. Graveer's muscular arms. "Boy, I almost didn't recognize you with those big guns!" He regarded his own thin, wasted, bruised arms. "I remember this being the other way around. I knocked you flat out at least a couple times!" He was laughing hysterically now.

"I'm going to leave now. Surgery is at 6 AM," Dr. Graveer said in a tense, clipped tone. He felt relieved that Hobart would be asleep when they met next.

"Wait! We're just starting to have fun! Remember when I poured anti-freeze into your locker? I wrecked your little blue sweater! You were quite a little runt back in the day!" He whistled. "But look at you now, all grown up and a high-powered surgeon with great big guns!" He was now visibly more short of breath between barks of laughter. "Well, I'll be! Oh, me!" he crowed.

Dr. Graveer's hand was on the sliding door now.

"Hey! Ain't karma something! I beat you up at least twenty-five times in school and now you get to cut me open tomorrow! Oh, me!" Tears of laughter were streaming down Hobart's cheeks now.

"I took an oath," Dr. Graveer rasped quietly as he left the room. He navigated the hallway in huge, rapid strides toward the elevator. He tried to deflect his thoughts as he entered the elevator: Lift weights. (Maybe a little punching bag work tonight, too). Lamb stew. Bed. Surgery at 6 AM.

Lift weights. Lamb stew. Bed. Surgery.

When Dr. Graveer arrived in the parking structure, he still could not redirect his thinking. As he drove, he began to picture a chess board. Yes, that was life. The same chess pieces being moved around in different combinations and configurations...

THE UNFINISHED BUSINESS OF FORGIVENESS

The winter chill was finally exiting the air on a late spring afternoon in Sault Ste Marie. I sat on a bench in Locks Park as was my usual lunch hour habit during the warmer months. I worked at a nearby art gallery where I also rented a small one bedroom apartment upstairs. My life was very well contained within a few blocks of downtown Sault Ste Marie.

A thousand foot freighter was downbound in the lock, horn blaring dramatically on the light breeze. In the twenty years since I'd been living here, I never tired of the drama of seeing the freighters transit through the Soo Locks. I could see shadows in the visitor's gallery waving to the men working on deck. The International Bridge to Sault Ste Marie, Ontario stood in majesty in the hazy distance.

The Soo Locks represented a true work of art or even a wonder of the world to me. I remembered seeing a photograph from the 1890s prior to the construction of the current locks. It is still in the visitor's center and bears the caption "Shooting The Rapids." Two women in winter coats are shown in a dangerously small boat, their fashionable hats of the times piled high on their heads and strapped securely at their chins. The women are laughing as they begin to transit the St. Mary's River, the men stoically seeing them off. I often wondered why they are laughing, given the peril of the experience. Is it the laughter of ignorance or nervousness? I also pondered how they looked at journey's end – likely soaked and potentially hypothermic at a minimum…maybe bruised, battered or worse at a maximum…

I noticed a woman milling about the chain link fence as the freighter began to leave the lock, horn still filling the air. She wore a light purple raincoat cinched at the waist and was hugging herself as if cold. She caught my eye and wandered over to the bench where I started eating an apple.

"Excuse me," she said softly. "May I sit?"

"Sure."

She quickly occupied the very end of the bench, more than a polite distance from me. She began rummaging through her purse and alternately squinting at the back of the departing freighter.

"Excuse me again," she said in a somewhat frustrated tone. "I can't seem to find my glasses in here. Can you see the name and location of the freighter?"

"Magnificent, it's called. It's from Milwaukee."

"Thank you," she added eagerly. Then, "Do you come here often?"

"All season," I replied. "It's my lunch hour routine. I work just down the block." To this point, I had only looked at her in cursory fashion, my eyes mostly on the downbound freighter. This was the very moment that I noticed her dark green eyes and the slight dimple in her cheek.

"Sharon."

I froze when she stated my name.

"Sharon, it's me. Elena." Her tone was almost pleading.

I bit deeply into the apple. Yes, it was definitely Elena. Twenty years older but still quite recognizable. Her face was thinner, bonier and more angular since our college days. Several strands of grey were beginning to creep into the crown of her brunette head, but it was unmistakably her. I couldn't fathom where to begin with her or what to say. I briefly closed my eyes, picturing those women of old "shooting the rapids."

Elena picked up the thread of the conversation. "Do you live here?" she asked timidly.

I had thoughts of simply getting up and walking away. I owed

Elena nothing. In fact, she owed me almost everything! But my lunch wasn't completed yet. I still had half of an apple and three carrot sticks. On the basis of this trivial fact, I decided to stay.

"Yes, I've lived here about twenty years. I work at an art gallery down the street. What about you?" The conversation had almost an elementary school "new friend" quality to it. "Where do you live?"

Elena gestured toward the International Bridge. "I'm in Canada," she replied vaguely. "I was teaching art at a secondary school but then I got sick. But now I'm back on my feet and I plan to return."

I nodded as I started on my carrot sticks. We were silent for a while. I could faintly hear the horn bleating on the departing "Magnificent." I wished I was on that freighter – anywhere but here.

Elena then broke the silence again. "You know, we didn't last, Rafie and I."

I cringed at her use of my pet name for Rafael, my college boyfriend and still the love of my life, despite everything.

As if sensing this, Elena continued, "After you left school, Rafael and I broke up about three weeks later."

I felt a surreally cold sense of comfort at that statement. My mind went back to my eighteen year-old self. I was beginning art school at Columbia University. It was the farthest I had been away from my home in Escanaba, Michigan. Everything about those first days was daunting.

Then I met Rafael Garza in the interminable line at student registration. I was pleased to learn that he was a fellow freshman, also in art school. His passion was sculpting, mine watercolors. I learned that he was also a long way from his home in southern Puerto Rico. Rafael was tall and string-bean thin with dewy brown eyes. His black hair hung to his shoulders and shook around as he spoke and laughed in animated fashion. It was the best wait in line I've ever experienced.

On that day, Rafael waited for me as I completed my registration. He had tied his long, luxuriant hair back into a loose man bun. He walked me to my dorm and politely bid me good night.

We became fast friends and soon we were an official item. Rafael's laugh and slightly broken English (complete with some hilarious malapropisms, I might add) captivated me instantly. He would dramatically unveil a new sculpture in my room. In my eighteen year-old mind, he was Michelangelo. My fellow art student and roommate Elena thankfully approved of Rafael as he was a frequent visitor. The three of us settled into an easy friendship – Rafael sculpting, me painting and Elena with her exquisite charcoal drawings.

Our romance grew exponentially. Time would seemingly evaporate. I loved sitting with Rafael on the front steps of the dorm as he described the scenic beauty of his homeland to me. "Beaches with sugar-like sand," he would say in a whisper. "I can't even describe the exact blue that the water is at home." Then, "I'll take you there someday." I loved the way he would critique my paintings. After a long period of sitting cross-legged on the floor with a furrowed brow, he would then stand up and gently point to each thing he loved in the work but with unbridled and animated commentary. He would sometimes be sweating with sheer enthusiasm after a critique!

I can't say exactly when, but a "shift" in our relationship occurred the following spring. Rafael became quiet when we were together. I missed "my chatterbox" and I told him so. His inner light and animated enthusiasm seemed to be gone. He insisted nothing was wrong, that he was just tired and a bit homesick. He also referenced a recent creative slump. I remember him telling me during this time that "Sometimes clay is just clay, nothing more. It just sits there in a lump. I can't bring anything out of it." I assured him in my girlish wisdom that all artists experience slumps but that the comeback is then all the more brilliant. I only elicited a half-hearted shrug in reply.

Around this time, Elena moved out. Her cousin had recently enrolled at Columbia and offered her a substantially larger dwelling with her own bedroom.

Rafael and I did a lot of long walks during this portion of our relationship. I was having to carry the entire conversation most days because he continued to be mired in silence. The clues were there, but I didn't see them.

One balmy night as we walked, I offered, "It was fun with the three of us at the movies last night. I can't believe that Elena has never seen a Hitchcock film!"

Rafael gave me his default shrug. "It's okay to be alone with you, too."

I stopped walking, parsing his words. Was he really saying that being alone with me was more of a "second best?"

Rafael stopped walking about five feet ahead of me.

Then I realized where we were. This was the dorm where Elena lived with her cousin.

I watched as Rafael looked up at Elena's brightly lit window. We then met each other's eyes sadly. We were done.

My attention popped back to the present. I was finishing the last carrot stick. I turned to Elena.

Elena's eyes were blurry with tears. "Can you forgive me, Sharon?"

Forgive her? I was incredulous.

Elena inched slightly closer to me on the bench. "Please forgive me, Sharon."

I swallowed. The carrot seemed to stick in my throat. My voice had a strangled quality as I responded to her. "I left school because of you guys," I managed. "I fell apart." I thought of my inglorious, broken return home to work at K-Mart in Escanaba prior to my decision to go north to Sault Ste Marie.

"I know, I know. And I'm sorry. We – I – didn't mean to hurt you!" she pleaded.

I stood and started packing my things. "I have to go. I'm already late in getting back to work!" I was being truthful – it was 1:10 and the gallery was supposed to reopen at 1:00. Without looking back, I walked briskly away from her.

"Wait, Sharon! Please forgive me! Then you can move on with your life!" she called after me.

I began to run, crossing the street and sprinting past the kitschy gift shops on my way back to the safety and sanctity of the gallery. "The nerve she has!" I thought. "The audacity!"

Three days later, I entered a more calm and reflective mode after an equal number of sleepless nights. Maybe Elena was correct. I needed to forgive her. It was on me that I left school and decided to wallow and then wall myself off.

I had conspicuously avoided all social media in my adult years as part of said "wall," but I combed the Internet to search for contact information for Elena. I used her maiden name, Fortuna, as I didn't know her marital status. She had gestured toward the International Bridge when I asked where she lived, simply stating "Canada." I began my search accordingly with Sault Ste Marie, Ontario. This yielded no results. I also came up empty on Facebook and several other social sites. I seemed to be at an impasse. I wondered if she would come to the park at the Soo Locks again – maybe that was my best bet...or...

Elena's mother! Yes, Priscilla! I still knew Priscilla's landline number in Albany from all the calls I placed to Elena during university breaks!

Priscilla answered on the second ring. I knew it was her immediately despite the passage of years – her Bristol, UK accent warmly entering my ear.

"Mrs. Fortuna, this is Sharon Engstrom. Do you remember me?"

A pause. Then, "Why, yes! Oh, Sharon! How are you?"

"Oh, I'm fine, Mrs. Fortuna." We proceeded to catch up a bit on the weather and my job at the art gallery. Finally, I said, "Listen, Mrs. Fortuna, this is really awkward, but I wonder if I could get Elena's contact information."

A longer pause ensued. Then, "Why?"

I sighed. "I want to forgive her for what happened with Rafael all those years ago. I ran into her in Sault Ste Marie and we talked-"

Priscilla took a sharp breath in. "What did you say?" She sounded shaky and very far away.

"I said that I saw Elena recently and-"

"When? When did you see her?"

"It was three days ago. Yeah, it would have been Monday noon."

The quiet on the other end of the line continued. I wondered if the connection had been lost. Then Priscilla came back on, "You say you spoke to Elena in person three days ago? On the twenty-first?"

"Yes." I was starting to feel like I was on the stand in court.

"Why, Sharon, I'm afraid that's quite impossible. Elena died seven months ago. She had metastatic breast cancer. I regret not seeing her more, but she lived all the way in Vancouver..."

I know that Mrs. Fortuna and I spoke for several more minutes but for me the real conversation ended right there.

Forgiveness. A simple word, but so elusive and damnably difficult in practice. Forgiveness. The time frame is limited, as transitory and fleeting as life itself.

THE SUPER FANTASTIC ULTIMATE BUCKET LIST WEEKEND

David had consumed enough Red Bull to fly into outer space during the all night poker tournament with his two besties. It was now 6:12 AM and all had decided that this would be the very last hand. (Although, they had also said the same at 2:18 AM and 4:36 AM).

David considered his cards as he also considered his two oldest and most faithful friends. There was Alan, a gentle giant with curly red hair and the build of a pro wrestler. Alan's brow was furrowed as he furtively rearranged the cards in his hand. Next to Alan was Rodrigo, razor-thin with short, coal black hair and a matching goatee. David himself resembled a surfer dude with his perpetual tan and wavy, shoulder-length blond hair with a bushy, mountain-man beard.

"Ready to call it?" Rodrigo was yawning.

"Read 'em and weep!" David slapped a full house – Aces and Kings – on Alan's kitchen table.

The "Aw, man!" exclamations were probably heard around the block, waking up the neighbors. David had virtually dominated the table all night.

"Go ahead! Gloat a bit! Count it!" laughed Alan.

David came up with $1,347.90 for the entire ten-hour extravaganza. Not bad!

"Are you sure you didn't miss your calling, dude? Maybe you should go on the poker circuit!" crowed Rodrigo.

David tossed his head back and laughed. The poker tournament was the first event in a weekend full of activities planned for David by Alan and Rodrigo. They had dubbed it "The Super Fantastic Ultimate Bucket List Weekend." On Monday morning, Alan would be taking David to the airport to depart for his new job.

The new job was to be all-consuming, to say the least. Hence, the elaborate send-off.

"Hey, let's get some breakfast!" said Rodrigo. "I'll pull my car around."

"Good plan," replied Alan. "I gotta pee!"

That left David sitting alone at Alan's kitchen table, staring at his spoils. He took a $50 bill off the top and tucked it into the pocket of his cargo shorts. Then he split the rest of the money between Rodrigo's stadium jacket hanging on the chair and a random drawer in Alan's kitchen.

Twenty minutes later, they arrived at Cosy's Diner right off the expressway. They requested a booth.

"We're going to need the biggest square footage you've got because we're going to eat this place out of business!" boomed Rodrigo.

The waitress' nametag read "Dottie." She looked at Rodrigo's string-bean physique. "I can hardly believe that!" she bantered. She threw a thumb over her shoulder at hulking Alan. "Now him, I could see some serious eating!"

They sat as Dottie circulated menus.

"So what's the biggest, most epic breakfast you've got?" Alan asked.

Dottie fished out her ordering pad and squinted in thought. "That would be the 'Maximum Overload'! It's a four-egg stuffed omelette with ten slices of bacon, a half pound of hashbrowns or American

Fries, three slices of ham and two of our homemade cinnamon rolls. Oh, and don't let me forget, a fruit cup!"

Alan fist-pumped the air, almost smacking Dottie. "Yes! Perfect!" he said. "Give that one to him!" He pointed at David.

Almost two hours later, they left Cosy's. David actually consumed 50% of his "Maximum Overload" before crying uncle. Then Alan picked up the slack to earn a clean plate award from the astonished Dottie. They headed back to Alan's apartment to get ready for the next event – ziplining.

David adjusted the strap on his ziplining helmet as he admired the beautiful river gorge. He found himself in a little reverie, in awe of God's creation. He wanted to imprint this gorgeous scene on his memory to retrieve in the times to come. He felt so far away that he didn't notice Alan joining him on the bridge.

Alan belched.

"Excuse you!"

"Yeah, I'm wondering if the timing of that epic breakfast could be problematic here!" Alan said this as he looked at the heights involved in the ziplining course.

"You didn't think that far ahead, didja bro?"

Alan's smile faded. "David, are you sure you want to do this?"

"Yeah! Ziplining is most definitely one of my bucket list items! I've been wanting to try it since I was a kid!"

"No, dude, I don't mean the ziplining. I mean the new job."

David paused. "I've never been more sure of anything ever before," he replied.

"Hey, they're calling us!" Rodrigo was motioning them over to the starting point.

"Too late to back out now!" David winked at Alan as they walked toward Rodrigo.

The weekend continued with mountain biking, a Cubs game and one of those restaurants where you stand around the barbeque and grill your own steak. By Sunday evening, David was pleasantly exhausted. He hoped for a good night's sleep as he set the alarm in Alan's spare bedroom. His flight was at 7:40 AM, so it would be an early call.

Alan appeared in the doorway. "Need anything, bro?"

"Nope. Hey, it was hard saying goodbye to Rodrigo."

"I guess that's life."

"Yeah, lots of meetings and partings."

"What car do you want to take to the airport tomorrow?"

"We can take mine," David said, thinking of his restored Jeep with the monster tires.

"Okay, good night." Alan turned to leave.

"Oh, and Alan? Thanks for everything. It was an awesome weekend. Really."

Alan smiled with visible sadness breaking through. "You're like my brother, you know that, right?"

David rose a bit earlier than he originally intended to take care of the grooming part. After completely shaving his head and beard, he considered his reflection. He looked so much younger this way, he thought – almost like being reborn. In a sense, this would come true later today.

David loaded his backpack with two sets of underwear, the same number of socks and a small plastic box containing his toothbrush. He also packed his beloved skateboard. He tossed his dirty clothes into Alan's washing machine and left a note in the spare bedroom to donate them to a homeless shelter.

"Ready, bro?" Alan had David's Jeep keys in his hand.

"I am," said David.

"Wow, you really look different. I can't believe it!"

David felt his newly smooth, cool scalp. "Part of the company dress code," he quipped.

At the airport, Alan pulled up to the curb. "Hey, we didn't talk about what to do with your Jeep."

"It's yours, buddy. Enjoy."

David landed in southern California later that afternoon. He proceeded to a cab but instructed the driver to let him out about a half mile from his final destination. David used the $50 from his poker winnings to settle the bill. He felt a sense of lightness in his being as he no longer had any money.

A quiet residential area preceded his destination. He was very pleased to see that the road sloped downward a bit. David removed the skateboard from his backpack and began soaring down the slope. It was a gorgeous early evening with a light breeze and gauzy, gentle sunlight. David was beginning to pick up speed. He laughed and closed his eyes, raising both hands in the air. He had never felt more absolutely free than he did in this moment.

David could see the building ahead, an austere-looking brick structure with a bell tower and a wrought iron fence. To his left was a modest ranch home with many children's toys haphazardly adorning the yard. David gently pushed his skateboard onto the grass, knowing the children would enjoy it. Now he had only the clothes on his back.

Then his hand opened the wrought iron gate. Then he was

walking up the ancient steps to the front door. He would live and die here. This was it.

The sign read "Order of Cistercians of the Strict Observance," the Trappist monks.

THE FLAPPER

I sat at my desk on a videoconference call. As CEO of Minneapolis Children's Hospital, I was looking forward to our annual fundraising dinner and silent auction. I would be attending with my wife, Barbara. This year featured a "Roaring '20s" theme. As I conferenced with our corporate events director, I felt an abiding pride and satisfaction with my career path. After twenty years as a pediatric otolaryngologist, I began climbing up the management chain. I felt more devotion than ever to our mission.

"So the silent auction items will be set up right at the entrance to the ballroom so guests don't get sidetracked and miss them." Kellie Buchler had been our corporate events director for the past seven years and she never failed to deliver an endless fount of creativity. She went on, smiling wryly at me on screen. "Of course, the champagne fountain and the chocolate fountain will both be stationed there to detain people for lengthy perusals of the auction items!"

I could feel my waistline expanding already as Kellie spoke. "A devilish but brilliant plan, Kellie!" I exclaimed.

"Thanks, Dr. Lemke."

"Kellie, please just call me Aaron."

"Okay, Aaron. Oh, and the band comes highly recommended. It's called 'Jazz Age.' They promise authentic 1920s style music, emphasizing lively jazz." Kellie held up a photo of the band members clad in white tuxedos with captain's hats and the conductor in a natty blue and white pinstriped suit.

I nodded. "Kellie, how are the guest numbers?"

"We're sold out. Four hundred fifty guests. That's all that the downtown Marriott ballroom will hold."

"Wonderful! Kellie, I'm sorry you won't be there this evening, but we'll talk tomorrow." Kellie would be assisting at a charity event for one of our affiliated hospitals in Rochester this evening.

"Well, have fun and cut the rug a bit, Aaron!"

"Will do! Bye."

We disconnected. The time was 5:50 PM. I looked at my tuxedo hanging in plastic on the inside of my office door. I closed the blinds and began to change into it. Barbara was meeting me here in twenty minutes so we could ride to the benefit together.

Dinner was lovely. The prime rib virtually melted in my mouth. I fondly regarded the guests at our table in the Marriott ballroom as the band belted out a Dixieland number. To my left was my wife of thirty years, Barbara. To my right was Dr. Manmeet Abdullah, Chief of Surgery. The seat next to him was unfortunately empty tonight. Dr. Abdullah's wife canceled at the last minute because she was not feeling well in favor of a movie night with her mother at home. He assured me that she was probably fine, just too uncomfortable to dance as she was now six months pregnant. Next to Barbara was Dr. Lea Fenn, Chief of Anesthesiology and her husband Gordon. Various other department heads and their guests populated the remainder of the table.

I almost hadn't recognized Dr. Abdullah on arrival that night. Instead of his usual chaotic hair, he sported tightly slicked-back locks in an attempt to look like a suave Jazz Age fellow. Dr. Abdullah savored his food and was typically the last one still eating. His eyes crinkled at the corners in pleasure as he consumed the final buttery bit of prime rib. I chuckled, remembering the same relish as he chowed on a dry donut at a staff meeting last week.

The band was now playing The Charleston. The dance floor immediately swelled with people. About fifteen seconds in, we noticed the crowd parting to accommodate a solo dancer. She was a young twentysomething and wore a sleeveless silk dress festooned with glittery jewels and sequins. She had a matching headband adorned with colorful feathers. Her makeup was heavy and exaggerated, especially the pink patches of rouge on her cheekbones and lipstick that looked like a pucker. Her legs whirled frenetically in a spot-on rendition of The Charleston.

"Wow, she's really good," commented Barbara. "That dance is all about the legs."

Dr. Abdullah was similarly captivated. "I've seen YouTube videos of The Charleston, but this one takes the cake!" he commented.

The woman's legs never stopped churning as the band roared. Most of the other dancers had stopped to watch. A spotlight focused on the woman's legs and then grew to two crisscrossing spotlights to showcase her performance. Periodically, her knees abducted at impossible angles.

Then the trombonist slid down the railing on the stage right staircase to join the woman on the dance floor. Despite these gymnastics, he did not miss a note! When he reached the woman, he swung the trombone high and low in huge arcs, almost as if the instrument was joining The Charleston.

Our entire table was now on its feet for a better view. The concluding applause was thunderous. I watched as the woman took an exaggerated bow, her huge string of pearls almost sweeping the floor. Then she reached up to the stage to retrieve her purse and starting making her way between the tables in the ballroom. She stopped here and there, ostensibly to accept compliments on her performance. Dr. Abdullah and I looked at each other in wonderment as she stopped next to the empty seat at our table. She placed a bejeweled purse with an ivory clasp on the table and withdrew a cigarette holder. I was fascinated because I had only seen these in old movies.

"Can anybody give a girl a light?" she said to no one in particular. She was standing about three inches from Dr. Abdullah's side. Her voice had the tinny but somehow booming resonance that I had also only heard in vintage films. Her diction was clipped and rapid with a slightly demanding but flirtatious tone, a la Mae West.

I cleared my throat. "Uh, ma'am, you can't smoke in the Marriott ballroom."

A thin sheen of sweat from her dancing effort was now visible. "Now that's a new one on me," she clipped, setting the cigarette holder on the table. Our group was chuckling and regarding her with rapt attention.

"Ma'am, would you like to join our table?" Dr. Abdullah gestured to the vacant seat next to him.

"My infinite pleasure!" she smiled, sitting immediately.

Barbara whispered to me, "You know, she's really, really good. Very authentic. She doesn't break character for even one second!" I nodded, noting to myself that all of us at the table had been born in the 1960s, so the Jazz Age was far from firsthand experience.

"What's your name?" Dr. Abdullah asked the woman.

"Sarah. Sarah Teasdale. Sarah COVINGTON Teasdale." She was clearly proud of her middle name in carefully accentuating it.

"Where are you from?" Dr. Lea Fenn was now speaking.

"I hail from Lynchburg, Virginia!" Sarah crowed proudly.

"Oh, you're part of the Bible Belt," Lea's husband Gordon commented.

"Not this gal, big boy!" Sarah shot back. This sent everyone at the table into laughter.

"You know, you are really good." My wife Barbara was now addressing Sarah.

"You just ask my mama about that! According to her, Satan has me by both ankles! What's good is the band! They're the bee's knees!" Sarah retorted.

"Dancing The Charleston must be good cardio," piped in Lea.

Sarah looked puzzled at this comment. Then she shrugged and turned to Dr. Abdullah. "Can a girl get a drink around here?"

"Sure!" Dr. Abdullah was already on his feet. "What can I get for you, Sarah?"

"Bourbon. With a glass of branch water."

Dr. Abdullah nodded. On his way up to the bar, he leaned down and whispered into my ear. "Aaron, what the heck is 'branch water'?"

"How would I know?" I whispered back. I clapped him solidly on the shoulder. "The bartender will know. Go on, my good man!" I said in my best imitation of clipped Jazz Age speech.

"My great grandmother had a purse just like that," Lea said, gesturing to Sarah's bejeweled bag. "Where did you get yours?"

"I've had it for ages, darling. I do know that I was vastly overcharged! Can you believe I paid an entire United States dollar for it!"

Lea and Barbara exchanged smiles.

"I enjoy thrift shop bargains myself," said Barbara. "Sometimes you can find vintage items for very little money."

Confusion clouded Sarah's face but by then Dr. Abdullah had arrived with her bourbon and branch water. We watched as she smoothly shotgunned both.

"Thank you, big boy!" Sarah beamed at Dr. Abdullah. "Now get me another! Dancing makes a girl thirsty!"

Dr. Abdullah obediently left the table to retrieve Sarah's second (and hopefully last) round.

"How long have you been dancing?" I asked Sarah.

She paused, a dreamy look in her eyes. Then she replied, "For all eternity, big boy. For all eternity."

After Sarah polished off another round of bourbon doused with branch water (Dr. Abdullah confessed to me that it was really from a bottle of Ice Mountain), our entire group hit the dance floor. Sarah's spectacular moves continued all evening long. At times, her legs seemed to levitate slightly above the dance floor they were moving so quickly. We never made it back to our table as the dancing took over all of us. My last glimpse of Sarah was of her doing a complete flip and then sliding on her knees for what seemed the entire length of the dance floor, her arms trailing behind her in blissful abandon.

When Barbara and I left (much too late at that), my tuxedo was actually sweated through.

The next morning, I sat at my desk videoconferencing with Kellie. Apparently the Rochester benefit had also been a solid success.

"The food was great. Putting the champagne and the chocolate fountains in the midst of the silent auction items was a brilliant idea," I told Kellie. "Whenever I looked over, that area was very busy."

"Great!" replied Kellie. "You gotta hit people where they live – their taste buds! How was the band?"

"Amazing!" I returned. "In fact, I'm actually sore from dancing. My tux shirt was completely pitted out at the end of the night!"

"Eeew!"

"Oh, and Kellie! I almost forgot! That roving flapper was sheer brilliance! She really made our night! She pretty much stole the show! She was so authentic! Where did you get her?" At first I thought the video had frozen because Kellie was stock still and silent.

"I'm sorry, what?" she finally managed.

"You know, the roving flapper! You should have seen it. She had Dr. Abdullah running up to the bar for her bourbon and branch water-"

"Aaron," Kellie interrupted. "I'm sorry. I don't know what you're talking about. I didn't hire any roving flapper for the benefit, although it sounds like an idea I should make a note of."

Now I hesitated. "So she wasn't a hired actress or performer? We all thought she was a plant."

"Aaron, could she have been a guest of someone? Was she with anyone?"

"She hung out with us and was on the dance floor quite a lot. I didn't see her with anyone."

Kellie's concerned expression deepened. "Let me look her up on the guest list. Did you get her name?"

"Yeah. It was Sarah. Sarah something. Sarah Teasdale, that's it! Sarah COVINGTON Teasdale, in fact. She said she was from Lynchburg, Virginia."

I waited as Kellie scrolled through the guest list. She looked up at me. "No such person on the list."

"Really!"

"Could she have been an alternate guest of someone else – maybe a last minute fill-in?"

"I suppose we'll never know, but you said yourself that the benefit was completely sold out. We only had one cancelation at our table because Dr. Abdullah's wife wasn't feeling well last night."

"Hmm." Kellie suddenly looked tired. "Well, looks like you had one heck of a party crasher there. No harm done, evidently, but I'll look into a better check-in and security system for future events. We lucked out this time, but we wouldn't want anything untoward happening at a fundraiser for Children's Hospital."

"Right on," I replied. "Hey, Kellie, what do the proceeds look like at present?"

"I should have better numbers for you later in the week, Aaron, but I expect they'll be impressive."

"Ah, good," I said contentedly, thinking of some of the many sorely needed capital budget requests.

"Okay, thank you, Aaron! Enjoy the day and an extra cup of coffee!"

"You, too, Kellie! Thank you for everything." I signed off, feeling the pain and tightness in my thighs from last night's exhaustive dance maneuvers. I was getting too old for late nights, no doubt.

I looked at the clock. I had a meeting with the hospital ethics committee in ten minutes. That gave me time to do a small Internet search. My fingers were poised and shaking slightly above the keyboard.

I already knew that I wouldn't find her on Facebook or Instagram or in the Twitter-verse. I went to a website that I seldom used but that a friend in the business had recommended. I slowly typed in "Sarah Covington Teasdale, Lynchburg, VA" in the search box.

The website was "Find a Grave.com."

POEMS

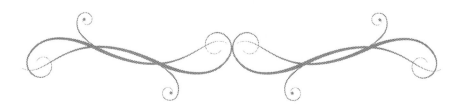

SUBCONSCIOUS

Like a locked door
You can pound, prod and kick all you want
But it won't open

When it opens, it BLOWS open
Like shafts of sunlight through a window
In a dark attic
Or lava exploding from a volcano
A dam
Bursting
Information billowing out
Like smoke from a wildfire

FATE

Fate is a speeding train
A discharged bullet
You cannot stop it
Try as you may
Immutable as stone
Unchangeable as gravity

DEBUSSY'S PIANO

When I hear Debussy's piano, I think of
A pastel pink sunset
Autumn leaves of scarlet red and honey gold in gauzy sunlight
Waves whispering and curling on the sand
Soft December rain
People reuniting in fond embrace
A mother beholding her infant adoringly
The young comforting the elderly

THE (SHORT-LIVED) SPLENDOR OF SNOW

Always more beautiful in sunlight
Or under stars
Or when you don't have to go anywhere

But snow does not age gracefully
It becomes ugly detritus
Has a short shelf-life indeed
Coating parking lots
Crusting curbs
All the better
To give way to the green carpet
Of spring

AUTUMN ODE

The weightless feeling of kicking into a thick pile of fallen leaves
The rich smell of cooling earth with tendrils of wood smoke
Gauzy sunlight as the daylight wanes into the depths of winter

JUMPERS TRIBUTE

Help could not reach you
So you helped yourselves
The choice was choking on smoke or being licked by flames
You chose to step out onto the fresh air

All we have left of you are shaky films and grainy photos
A woman modestly holding down her billowing skirt
A cook plummeting torpedo-style, arms stoically at his sides

FDNY said there were so very many of you
Dropping like thunderclaps or gunshots

Amen, to all of you
Oh, for a sip of fresh air!
You glided right into God's soft, waiting arms

DREAMS

AUTHOR'S NOTE: The following pages are accounts of dreams I have had during the course of the COVID-19 pandemic. I have made every attempt to record each dream precisely as I remember it. There are two approaches to reading these dreams: (1) Read with an interpretation in mind – a lesson, a moral, a symbol or maybe an allegory. (2) Read strictly for entertainment, as you would a piece of fiction. The choice is yours! Remember to suspend belief even a little bit more than usual as you take a ride on the subconscious!

LEAVING
THE TEA HOUSE

My husband Bob and I were in Jamaica at a resort we had previously stayed at many times. We were walking hand in hand on the resort grounds. I noted that much tropical foliage had been cleared since our prior visit in favor of broad concrete walkways. Colorful murals had also been added to many of the lodging villas. I wore a peasant blouse with puffy sleeves and jeans. Bob wore jeans with a hoodie.

"There's a great place to get a burger. It's right on the ocean. We've been there before," Bob said.

I frowned. As this was an all-inclusive resort, I only recalled eating at the restaurants on the property. However, I looked forward to trying something new.

Then we were at the oceanfront. We saw a Japanese tea house. It was actually built on the water with no floor. You could step right into it from the pier. It contained two very high chairs that were somehow anchored underwater. It occurred to me that this would be a great place to cool off in the shade and dangle one's legs in the water. A battered rowboat was also floating in the tea house.

"Go in," Bob said.

"Is just anyone allowed in?" I countered, suspecting that this curious structure was private property.

Bob insisted it was okay for us to enter. I wanted to sit on one of the high chairs but Bob directed me to sit in the rowboat.

The next thing I knew, I was floating out of the tea house onto the open water. I felt helpless and embarrassed. I called out to Bob who was standing on the pier. By now, a uniformed policeman was also standing on the pier next to Bob with a disgusted look on his face.

"Ma'am, you've got to steer!" the policeman shouted to me across the water.

There was one problem. Bob was holding the oars. They were in two pieces and thus had not even been assembled.

I had thoughts of asking Bob to throw me the oar when the policeman cried out again: "Lady, you're going to crash!"

Startled, I looked over my shoulder to see that the rowboat was rapidly approaching a power boat tethered to an adjacent pier. The owner was putting gas into the power boat calmly.

I turned around to look at Bob on the other pier when suddenly the rowboat started heading back in the direction of the tea house. I'm thinking that the power boater probably (and thankfully) gave me a push in the right direction.

"That's much better, lady!" shouted the policeman. "That's what I'm talking about!"

12-17-20

THE DOG AND
HIS REFLECTION REDUX

My husband Bob and I stood on a sandy expanse that could have been a boat or canoe launch overlooking a river on a sun-dappled afternoon. Sandbars ran along each side of the river.

I then saw a jewelry box floating relatively close to the sandbar on one side of the river. I was immediately intrigued. What if it contained something valuable? I was suddenly and singularly obsessed with finding out.

Without consulting Bob, I jumped into my Ford Focus and began driving along the generous sandbar. My plan was to stop parallel to the jewelry box and reach for it from the car so as not to get wet. My plan worked swimmingly. In moments, I had opened up the car door and retrieved the jewelry box. I then left the car and began walking toward Bob back on the boat launch area.

"Look!" Bob cried.

I whirled around. My car had somehow slid laterally on the sandbar and was now sinking into the river. Half of the front grille was already submerged and the back end was slightly up in the air.

With trembling hands, I opened the jewelry box. It was empty.

12-25-20

JACKPOT:
ALWAYS THE GROOM

My hotel window on one side faced a recreational path that wound through the complex and into the neighboring community. Hotel patrons could regularly be seen walking or jogging along with parents pushing strollers or elderly couples strolling. One patron of the path that stood out in my mind was the man wearing the grey tuxedo and tails. I saw him from my window several times a day, usually with two children on bikes who appeared to be about five and seven years old respectively. The man would attentively spot and steady them on the bikes as both children were at that wobbly stage in their riding skills. He was ostensibly escorting them to and from school, always with a gentle smile on his face. Sometimes I would see him strutting happily down the path alone, always in his tux and tails, chin thrust proudly into the air. He had blond curly hair, sparkling blue eyes and a patchy blond slacker-type beard.

One day I saw him again with the two children on their bikes. The girl's bike was adorable with pink streamers on the handlebars. Curiosity then got the better of me. I flung open the window and called out to him.

"Excuse me!"

He stopped and looked up at me, briefly pointing both thumbs at himself as if saying, "You mean me?"

"Yes, you!"

He smiled endearingly up at me.

"What's with the tux all the time?"

The man looked down at his tux and tails as if first noticing them. "You see," he began. "I hit the jackpot! I have a beautiful wife and two healthy, wonderful kids. So I decided to always be the groom!" He then gave me a friendly wave and ran off to catch up with the children.

I closed the window. I couldn't help myself. I started clapping.

12-27-20

MURDERESS/
MURDEROUS

She was standing on a small bridge over a stagnant pond at dawn. Fog was rising from the water giving it an ethereal look. She pulled the wrinkled paper bag from her coat pocket and pulled out the gun. She handled it with only the tips of her fingers as if it was an odious thing.

She thought she may have killed someone last night. She was not completely certain because she did not remember specifics other than the presence of the gun.

She leaned over the bridge and dropped the gun into the still water, surprised at how quietly and seamlessly it landed. She watched the little whorls and rings fade on the surface of the water as the gun settled onto the murky bottom. Then she went home and got ready for work, eager to maintain normalcy. She washed and styled her hair. She donned dress pants, a sky blue blouse and a black blazer. She felt better already as she looked in the mirror.

She arrived at her job in a large, windowless office complex in an unnamed industrial park. She was promptly greeted by the receptionist with "Someone from the FBI is here and would like to speak with you." ("Wow!" she thought. "That was quick!") She wended her way down the bright fluorescent-lit corridor to the conference room.

The conversation with the FBI man was short and cordial. Largely boilerplate stuff. Where were you last night? (Home. Sleeping). Can anyone verify that? (No, she was alone all night. She texted a few friends before bed, but she guessed that didn't count). At the end of the interview, the FBI man said he would be in touch with further questions and left her with a four-page form to fill out and fax to him immediately upon completion. After he left, she remained in the conference room to complete the paperwork, which ended up being a reiteration of the items in the interview plus some biographical information.

She was standing at the fax machine sending the form when the receptionist approached her again. She looked at her watch, noting that it was already 9:45 AM and she hadn't performed any job-related duties.

"There's a second person from the FBI here to see you," said the receptionist as if this were the most uneventful morning in the history of the office.

Her thoughts repeated themselves: "Wow! That was quick!"

On shaky legs, she entered the conference room once again to encounter a different FBI man. He was not cordial like his colleague but rather brusque and almost menacing. She repeated her story to his dour, accusatory expression. Then he removed two photographs from his suit pocket. "Do you know either one of these men?" he asked.

She regarded the photos. One of them looked like a prisoner in a mugshot. The other was actually a photo of a large boulder. "I don't know the man, but, with all due respect, sir, I don't see a person in the second photo," she said timidly.

The questioning then came to a close and she was dismissed. The FBI man remained seated as she stood to leave.

"Oh, and Miriam?" He called out to her as she reached the door. "Yes?"

He looked her dead in the eye. "You will be going down for this. It's just a matter of time. Once we find the gun, the bullets in the victim's body can be matched to it."

HOSPITAL-BOUND: POSSIBLE SAN DIEGO CONDITION

I was printing something from my computer when my mom entered the room.

"Susan," she said in a concerned tone. "The doctor wants additional testing. You may have the 'San Diego Condition' at the entrance to your stomach."

I was thoroughly puzzled. Additional testing? I didn't remember any initial testing. Furthermore, I wasn't having any untoward stomach symptoms. And what in the world was the "San Diego Condition?"

My mom meant business. She was clutching what looked like hospital registration papers in her hand...

1-7-21

STOOD UP

I received a phone call out of the blue from Oleg, a high-school acquaintance whom I had not seen since 1982. He had heard that I was attending the "Important Conference" in Washington, D.C. He stated that he would also be attending and offered to drive me to the airport on departure day. I quickly said yes, thinking of previous parking hassles at the airport. It was a pleasant but vague conversation.

On the morning of my flight to the "Important Conference," I packed a small duffel bag. I liked the wide shoulder strap for carrying because I didn't plan to check any baggage at the airport. The master bedroom where I was packing resembled my girlhood bedroom but the rest of the house was exactly like my late mother's bi-level condo. The subdivision outside also corresponded to my late mother's condo development.

I walked into the kitchen, duffel bag on my shoulder. My late mother and father were both there, along with multiple other anonymous people. I felt sharp in my best business-casual blazer. My parents wished me well at the "Important Conference."

I walked out onto the driveway. Our flights were at 11:00 AM and it was now 9:35 AM. Oleg would be here any minute. Fifteen minutes passed and no Oleg. I decided my duffel bag was a bit too heavy and that I would return indoors for a moment to revisit my packing and perhaps eliminate some unnecessary items. After all, I would only be gone for two days. And surely Oleg would honk his horn or come to the front door when he arrived.

Back in the master bedroom, I unloaded some superfluous documents and secured them in the chest of drawers. The duffel bag already felt lighter. Then I realized that the drawers needed better organization so I tended to that. Satisfied with my work, I checked my watch. 9:55 AM. I went to the window and peered out. Still no Oleg.

I walked back out onto the driveway and pulled out my cell phone. No messages. I replayed my cordial but brief phone conversation with Oleg in my mind. Wait – had I ever gotten his contact information? Had he asked for my address? My eyes locked onto my car. It was now 10:00 AM, straight up. As I entered my car, I decided in advance to forward the speeding ticket I would likely get on my way to the airport to Oleg.

1-9-21

ACKNOWLEDGMENTS AND DEDICATIONS

To my precious husband, Bob Knier. You will always be my first audience!

To my wonderful uncle, Bill Hayes. Thank you for being such a good brother to my late mother. I admire your strength, resilience and intelligence.

To Juanita Smith and Mary Williams, wonderful caregivers to my late mother and equally wonderful friends. Juanita: I love singing at the top of my lungs with you. Mary: I love your stories about Vegas. Shout out to Dynasty and Vernon, too!

To my fun-loving brother-in-law, the late Terry Knier. We will definitely see you again.

To God. Thank you for ushering us safely through 2020 and for teaching us what is most important.

Printed in the United States
By Bookmasters